by Kris Felstehausen

A Native American village nestled in the valley of a low range of mountains in the mid 1700's...

One man wrestles with what he fears is a terrible truth... one that shakes the very foundation of his world.

Another man blindly follows his greed and jealousy to a tragic end.

Each has a secret...

Felste LearningWorks, LLC

FelsteLearningWorks.com

Published by:

Felste Learning Works, LLC
Palatine, IL 60074
FelsteLearningWorks.com

Felste Learning Works
527 E. Thornhill Ln
Palatine, IL 60074
www.felstelearningworks.com

ISBN-13: 978-1539425342
ISBN-10: 1539425347
First Edition, November 2016
Printed in the United States of America

To my husband Norbert
for all his love, encouragement, and support

Map

N

W E

S

North Forest
and Meadow

Tribal Village
with Council House

Tanawha
Mountain

Standing Rocks

Great Oak
near Southern Pass

Characters & Terms

Ahyoka: Kisosen's granddaughter; 'she brought happiness'

Chaska: Kisosen's son; name given to first-born son

Ghigau: the village chief's wife; 'beloved woman'

Goosefoot (aka Chenopodium): a plant producing starchy seeds and spinach-like greens

Hashi: the sun

Hialeah: Kisosen's daughter-in-law; 'beautiful meadow'

Itanale: Kisosen's given name; 'I understand'

Kisosen: (Kee-zos-en) the sun bringer

Losa: a man in the village; 'black'

Malili: a man in the village; 'he runs'

Mali humma: the story antagonist; 'blow red'

Onsi: a man in the village; 'eagle'

Pemmican: a concentrated mixture of fat and protein used as a nutritious food

Pigweed (aka amaranth): an annual leafy green vegetable

Shotek: Mali humma's son; 'sky'

Sofkee: a gruel similar to hominy grits

Sumpweed: 5 foot tall herb that produces many small flower heads in a narrow, elongated, spike-like array, each head with 11-17 disc florets

Tanampi: Mali humma's brother; 'to be hostile; to be at war'

Tarn: small mountain lake

Yanegwa: the chief of the village; 'big bear'

Zamia root: like a turnip

Chapter 1

He stood on the east side of Tanawha Mountain. Even though dark, he could still see his breath. He was waiting... waiting for the right moment to awaken Hashi.

He stood like the tree, with deep roots, powerful trunk, and great spreading branches that reached to the sky.

> *Great and powerful Hashi,*
> *Awaken so we may honor you this day*
> *and thank you for your gifts.*
> *You are the light over the crops,*
> *the heat that warms the earth,*
> *the hope that springs eternal,*
> *the bringer of life.*
>
> *Strengthened by your gifts,*
> *I avail myself to the force of the Universe*
> *to guide you from your bed.*
> *In motion I soar like the eagle.*
> *In quietness I am like the hibernating bear.*

At least, that's what he told his mind. He did not feel strong or soaring anymore, though. He felt old, and tired, and cold.

He was the Kisosen, the bringer of Hashi. As the oldest male in his family line, it was his duty to rouse Hashi from her sleep each morning and put her to bed each night.

As a boy, fulfilling this honor was his only desire. He was consumed with longing as his grandfather and then his father climbed the mountain each evening and returned each morning after effecting their duty. He yearned for the day when the people of the village would greet him with "Praise to Kisosen for Bringing Hashi to Nourish and Protect."

As he waited, trying to find his strength, a bitter chill nipped at his ears. He wished he had his beaver fur hat. Damn! He must concentrate. He must focus. Each day it seemed harder to find the energy to wrench Hashi from the soil.

The doubting whisper was back. It came every morning since "It" happened. Disguised by the whistling wind, it whispered cruelly in his ear: "It doesn't really matter. You are not the one awakening Hashi."

But then, there - like a spade piercing the soil - the first glimmer of light pushed up from the darkness, blushing like a timid maiden. He smiled. It would be okay. He gulped down his doubt. He would reason with "It" another day.

Chapter 2

The climb down Tanawha Mountain each morning was easier than the climb up each evening. He knew every twist and bend in the trail, every loose rock, every shady stop along the way. After the long and solitary sleep in his mountain hut, he breathed deeply taking in the crisp, easy morning air. As he descended, the Red Spruce and Fraser Fir gave way to oak, hickory, and red maple. Off to his right reverberated the sound of a snapping twig as a large animal paced through the trees. Deep red bee balm wobbled in the breeze and the herbal scent of yarrow tickled his nose. Hashi warmed the top of his head as she climbed higher in the morning sky.

The village lay in a protected valley along the Great River surrounded by smaller relatives of Tanawha Mountain. It was much warmer in the valley with a morning breeze playfully teasing the leaves of the dogwood, witch hazel, and mountain laurel. Hashi's painted strokes were just beginning to color the petals of the lily of the valley, spoonleaf sundew, bellwort and goldenrod. Kisosen pause to listen to the songs of the Wood Thrush and Tufted Titmouse warning that it would be another warm day. As Hashi made her climb to the top of the sky, she grew agitated with the effort and spewed her fervor on the village.

At the center of the village was a large, pebble-covered plaza with a central hearth and benches for tribal gatherings and ceremonies. Chief Yanegwa's Council House dominated the east side of the plaza, it's round stone walls and domed thatched roof wrapping protectively around the Most Beloved Man and his family. The Great River lay to the west. Smaller, round family huts made of saplings covered with bark and animal skins squatted obediently around the Council House. Bordering the huts and ending at the river on both the north and south sides of the village, was a rugged, eight-foot high palisade fashioned of small and medium-sized tree trunks driven deep into the ground and honed to a point at the top. The southern gates were thrown open wide to welcome Kisosen and allow a smooth exit for those assigned to gather roots, wild blueberries, crab apples and nuts, or to hunt for white-tailed deer, fish, wild turkeys, raccoons, and bear. Immediately outside the palisade were the tribal fields of corn, beans, squash, pumpkins, sunflowers, and many other crops.

The smells of pemmican, sofkee, honey, and a sweet-tasting bear fat sauce wafted on the morning breeze as Kisosen made his way to his family's hut for breakfast. He was more than famished from the long climb down Tanawha Mountain.

As he ducked through the door he was greeted by Hialeah's encouraging smile. He immediately spotted, at the neck of her poncho-style blouse, the carved bone broach he had made for her last winter. Her deerskin wrap-around skirt showed the bulge of his second grandchild. She had combed her shiny black hair with bear grease and pulled it into braids adorned with bone and stone beads. She bowed her head in greeting and motioned for him to sit by the fire where his bowl of sofkee and pemmican waited, prepared just to his liking.

As he sunk down wearily next to the fire, letting the warmth settle into his bones, he heard the bright chatter of Ahyoka coming closer, her voice light, and joy diffusing all around her. Chaska slipped into the hut pulling the chattering child by the hand.

"Grandfather!" Ahyoka exclaimed, her brown, almond-shaped eyes dancing joyously. "You have come at last! Why are you so late? We were about to come looking for you."

"Ahyoka, show your respect." admonished Hialeah.

"Oh sorry..." bowed Ahyoka with a flush of embarrassment. "Thank you great Kisosen for bringing Hashi to us this morning." Kisosen bowed his head in acknowledgment, but more to hide the doubt he was sure must seep from in his eyes.

"Ahyoka, leave your grandfather in peace. It is time for the morning wash." Hialeah motioned for her to help gather the breakfast bowls. "Come with me to the river. Your father and Kisosen have much to discuss."

Chaska pulled back the buckskin door to the hut as Hialeah and Ahyoka, arms laden with soiled bowls and the hominy pot, set out for the river. Once their footsteps died away, a heavy silence settled in the hut. Kisosen could tell that his son was wrestling with his thoughts, wondering how to phrase the question he clearly wanted to ask.

"Father," Chaska sunk down to Kisosen's right, but turned so he could look him in the eye. He had high cheekbones and a broad, hooked nose resembling the curved beak of an eagle. "I am worried. You seem... distant. Distracted. Sorrowful?" He shifted his gaze to stare into the glowing embers of the breakfast fire. "I have not seen you this way since mother took flight to the next world."

A heavy and onerous silence stretched between them. Kisosen struggled with his thoughts. What should he say? How do you disclose doubt without creating fear? How do you question your family's heritage and purpose? How do you shatter a belief without shattering the soul?

"Maybe I should come with you to Tanawha Mountain tonight... for a few nights? Maybe it's time for me to learn more of the secrets of managing Hashi?" Chaska's let his words hang in the air and tumble into the bends and folds of the hut.

Kisosen pursed his lips and let out a long breath. He stared at his crooked pinky finger. It seemed that several minutes elapsed before he answered. "Some secrets cannot be shared, but must be learned through a long and difficult journey."

But as soon as the last word had left his lips, Kisosen realized with a stabbing flash that those were the words of his father. Spoken to him when he asked the same question many years ago. Is this what his father had meant? Is the secret really a falsehood that his father was too weak to reveal? That he is now also too weak to reveal? Or is this the difficult part of the journey - the struggle and self-discovery - that his father knew he must endure to truly become the bringer of Hashi?

Kisosen became aware that his son was staring at him. He raised his gaze to meet his only son's dark, heavy-lidded eyes. An unspoken message flashed between them, then Chaska looked down and away. "Forgive my disrespect, Father. I have faith that you will tell me when it is time."

A moment passed where they listened to the dying crackle of the fire and the distant voices of the villagers as they called to each other to greet the morning and plan the work of the day. Chaska squirmed uncomfortably struggling to find a way to change the subject and continue the conversation.

"Last night, after you left for the mountain," Chaska said with relief, "Mali humma and his brother were in very bad temper. He was most disrespectful to Chief Yanegwa."

"What was it this time?" sighed Kisosen. "The same thorn? Or has he found a new trouble to let fester?"

Chaska grunted with irritated resignation. "He disagrees with the tribe's decision to trade with the white settlers. He wants to show them the points of our arrows instead of our furs and deerskins. He thinks we have no use for their iron pots, woven fabrics, or their whiskey." Chaska puffed up his chest and donned an expression mimicking the ill-tempered villager. "He said, 'Those who deal with the white devil will see the devil themselves!'"

"Did you show your support for the chief?"

"Yes, Father. Onsi, Malili, Losa, and I stood brave and strong behind Chief Yanegwa! We showed Mali humma and Tanampi that they are alone in their short-sighted ways."

"What about Shotek?" Kisosen asked.

"He is without spirit! He cows to his father's and uncle's wishes without question or reason. He slouched behind his father like a coward!"

Kisosen looked deeply into the fire and sucked in a long breath. "His father's anger is a burden that has rounded Shotek's shoulders, withered his judgement, and buckled his spirit." Kisosen shifted his gaze and locked eyes with his son. "I do not think Shotek agrees with his father, though. Could you live with a man like that and still be whole?" Chaska sat back, wrapped his arms around his knees, and rocked back deep in thought.

Kisosen continued, "Mali humma wants to be the chief, but the hate pours from him like a mighty waterfall, drowning everything in his path. A chief should hold his people's heads above the water, not pull them under."

"True. So, true." Chaska blew out a worried breath. "I wonder, though, if Chief Yanegwa is strong enough to tame this 'waterfall.'"

Before Kisosen could answer, the lively voice of Ahyoka gossiping excitedly with her mother announced their return from the river. Ahyoka burst through the door of the hut holding the door flap open for Hialeah who was balancing the washed and dried dishes and pots.

Hialeah's brown eyes met her husband's asking her silent question. He gave her a tiny nod, then rose from his place by the fire. "I must go and join the hunt. I will be back for the evening meal."

Hialeah motioned to the bundle she had prepared. "Don't forget your mid-day meal. I have packed jerky, pemmican, and some fruit and nuts to sustain you on the hunt."

"Thank you." Chaska wrapped his arms around his wife in a warm and loving embrace. "I am a lucky man to have such a good woman."

Chaska drew his woven possum hair belt around his trim and muscular waist. The food bundle disappeared into the deer skin pouch that hung from his belt and in front of his buckskin breechcloth. A knife of flint with a carved bone handle was also securely fastened to the belt.

He then donned leather chaps that went from the ankle to mid-thigh and fastened them with thongs to his belt. The chaps would protect his legs during the hunt. His course black hair was pulled back into a topknot. He picked up his bow and threw a strap over his shoulder that held a bag with arrows, cane stalk blowgun, and blow darts dipped in poison. With his bow, Chaska could fell a deer with deadly accuracy from 100 yards away.

As Chaska left for the hunt, Hialeah turned to Kisosen. "The first harvest of beans are ripe and must be picked. Ahyoka and I are going to the fields. We could use your help if you feel up to it."

Kisosen struggled to his feet and stretched his aching back. "Yes, I will help. It will do me good to bask in Hashi's glow."

Chapter 3

As Kisosen walked through the village toward the fields, he was greeted by groups of women and girls grinding corn into corn meal or making paluska holbi or bunaha. Paluska holbi was a bread made by pouring boiling water into cornmeal, shaping the stiff dough into small rolls, wrapping the rolls in cornhusks, and then cooking them under hot ashes. Kisosen preferred the bunaha. It was a mixture of dried beans, wild potatoes, and cornmeal, shaped into rolls, wrapped in cornhusks, and boiled in water. Some women and children were also braiding cornhusks into sleeping mats, baskets, and dolls.

The first harvest of long-eared, multi-colored corn that had been picked over the last week lay drying in great mounds upon mats in front of each hut. After drying, the corn kernels were shelled from the cobs and sealed in corn cribs suspended atop seven foot posts. The posts were polished so that the mice could not climb them and eat the corn. The cribs were lined with grasses to prevent mildew or spoiling. When corn was needed, the seal on the door was broken, corn removed, and the door resealed. The leftover cobs and husks were burned for fuel.

Many other villagers were heading out to the fields to pick ripe crops, hoe weeds, or plant new crops. The tribe had built scaffolds spaced evenly throughout the fields where elderly women sat and watched for crows and rabbits. They would shake bottle gourds filled with pebbles to scare predators away. At night, the men and older boys would take turns patrolling the fields to keep nocturnal animals away.

The tribe's plantings stretched for a mile along the river on both the north and south sides of the settlement. Over many generations, the tribe had learned to plant their corn and beans in small hills spaced about three feet apart, laid out in long, straight lines running north to south to maximize Hashi's light. The corn was planted first and the beans several weeks later. This way the vines of the climbing beans could twine themselves around the cornstalks, and the bushy leaves of the beans provided shade to keep the corn's roots cool and protected. Through trial and error, the tribe discovered that corn and beans formed a good marriage. The two crops always thrived when planted together and seemed to struggle when kept apart. In between the mounds were planted other crops including white bush scallop squash, sweet potatoes, reddish-orange pumpkins, sumpweed, goosefoot, bottle gourds, pigweed, and purple tomatoes. Sunflowers edged the north end of each field.

At the northern palisade gate, Ghigau, the chief's wife, was handing out river cane and cornhusk baskets for collecting beans and other crops. As Ghigau handed Kisosen a basket, he smiled and bowed his head in respect. She returned his smile flashing her large front teeth. Her round, broad, bronze-colored face was lined and weathered from a lifetime of working in the sun. Her hair was pulled back in a bun and decorated with beads. To show her status as most beloved woman, she had brightly colored feathers arranged in an intricate pattern in the fringe of her tanned and softened deerskin skirt.

Kisosen made his way to the far end of the northern field. He did not feel like talking or listening to the constant chatter and gossip of the women, children, and other elderly men working the fields. He wanted only solitude to mull over his earlier conversation with Chaska.

He turned his face up toward Hashi and breathed deeply in and out, taking in the mid-morning air. Looking around he picked through the individual mounds of corn and beans until he found a plant with green, 6 inch-long pods sporting a purplish overlay that signaled an interior of ripe, shiny, jet-black beans. He began using his fingernails to pinch the pods off just shy of their junction with the vine, pulling the pod away carefully to leave the pod strings attached to the vine. This would save time later as the pods would not need further destringing.

As he worked and Hashi climbed higher in the sky, he lowered himself to the earth, seeking the shade of the cornstalks, and began picking the beans that lay closer to the ground. He was suddenly overcome with fatigue and rubbed his hands slowly up and down his creased and weathered face. After lunch, he decided, he would go to the north meadow and find a secluded spot to take a nap. The meadow was peaceful. He could sleep there. He must chase away the deep weariness that saturated his bones. He could no longer sleep through the night. After putting Hashi to bed he would fall exhausted onto his mat and into a restless sleep devoid of dreams or replenishment. He would awaken terrified in the middle of the night, tossing and turning, agitated and weary. He would fight to calm his mind, his fears, telling himself to have faith - that he will awaken in time - that he will fulfill his duty, but sleep would not find him. He must find some resolution! He could not continue this way. Maybe Chaska was right. Maybe he should turn the duty over to him. He was younger, stronger - his faith deep and unshaken. But... he was still so young. It was a great burden to hang on such fresh, contented shoulders.

The sounds of shaking gourds and calls to the mid-day meal that traveled from woman to woman throughout the fields roused him from his anxieties. He struggled to his feet hefting the half-filled basket of beans. 'A pitiful effort!' he thought, looking at his small yield. He could not even do this well. He was useless!

The field workers streamed back into the village through both the north and south gates gathering in the central plaza around the central fire. The women of the village took turns, working in small groups, to prepare the mid-day meal. Two lines were formed, one on each side of the fire, to receive a hearty scoop of succotash, a tasty vegetable dish made of corn, beans, and squash. Sassafras tea was poured freely from bottle gourds, mounds of berries and nuts sat heaped on mats for the taking.

Kisosen settled resignedly in his place on the east, central bench closest to the fire. This bench was reserved for him, Chief Yanegwa, and the village shaman. Hialeah brought a cup of tea and bowl of succotash to Kisosen, dropping to her knees in front of him out of respect. She laid her young, strong hand on Kisosen's knee and looked sympathetically into his tired eyes. "What else can I bring you?"

Before he could answer, though, a flash of movement distracted Hialeah. She glanced quickly around scanning the crowd for Ahyoka. When she saw the frisking child dodging excitedly between tribal members in a game of tag with her friends, she called admonishingly to her, "Ahyoka! Bring your grandfather some berries. Sit down and eat! There will be time for fun later." She arose in a fume, darting after her impish child, light on her feet even with the added weight of her growing child.

Kisosen let loose a long breath and took a deep drink of the tea. It was strong and cool from the deepest part of the river waters. He hadn't realized how thirsty he was. Another woman from the tribe saw that his cup was empty and quickly refilled it. He bowed his head in thanks and drank again. As he slowly ate his succotash the chatter and gossip of the tribal members surrounding him began to swirl together into an indistinguishable prattle. His mind seemed to travel away down a quiet tunnel to a secret place. A silent, dark place - where he stood alone - surrounded by the rush and energy of others, but not a part of it.

"Grandfather! Are you listening to me?" Kisosen was suddenly roused by small hands shaking his knees. His eyes regained their focus to find a newly made cornhusk doll shaking excitedly a hand's breath from his face. Ahyoka's dark and lively eyes were dancing with life and energy as she rocked the doll from side to side to show off her new treasure.

"This is Acheba! Do you know what she told me?" Ahyoka said in a tumble of eagerness. "Last week she was snuggled around an ear of corn. Her life was most delightful! She would sway in the breeze and feel Hashi's warmth on her skin. She felt the rain fall on her head and tickle her silks." Ahyoka swayed back and forth while trickling her fingers down her shiny black hair mimicking an ear of corn swaying in the breeze and enjoying an early summer rain.

"But then she was scared!" Kisosen could not help but chuckle as Ahyoka snapped together, making herself small with her arms wrapped protectively around her narrow shoulders and began to shake uncontrollably with imagined fear. "She heard her sisters and brothers cry out in fear as they were ripped away from their mother!" At this Ahyoka donned a cruel and angry sneer as she mimed the actions of a villager pulling ripe ears of corn from the stalk.

"All of a sudden, she was ripped from her mother and thrown into a basket! Other ears of corn were thrown on top of her. She couldn't breathe! All the other ears were crying around her. But she was brave! She did not cry."

"I see," said Kisosen softly. "That means she is very strong." He reached out and took the doll gently in his hands turning her slowly to see Ahyoka's handiwork. "Then what happened?"

Ahyoka, delighted at the attention, pressed on with her story. "After what seemed like half the day..." she leaned over and whispered covertly into Kisosen's ear, "...because it was - she was dumped onto a mat with her brothers and sisters and lay quietly in front of our hut. At first she tried to make herself very small so no one would take notice of her. Do you know what, though?" Ahyoka pressed her small and lively face close to Kisosen's. "She told me she was watching me for several days trying to decide if I was nice and would be her friend!" She rocked back on her heels and crossed her arms in mocked insult. "Then she finally decided to take a chance and started calling out to me. I heard her tiny, little voice this morning. Ahyoka!" she mimicked a high squeaky voice, "Ahyoka! Bring me happiness! Make me your friend!"

Ahyoka scooped the doll from Kisosen's hands and held her up high in the air glowing with pride. "So I found her, freed her from her ear of corn, and shaped her into this lovely doll. And now she is very happy!" Ahyoka hugged the doll to her chest bending her head over her with pleasure. "And so am I."

Kisosen smiled warmly at his granddaughter and gently clapped his hands together in appreciative applause. "That was a wonderful story, Ahyoka. You have learned well from Chief Yanegwa. You will make a fine wife and mother someday." He lovingly tickled his fingers under her chin and ran his old, tired hand down her loose, shiny black hair.

An angry snarl from across the plaza shattered the harmonious exchange and the entire tribe's repose following the meal. Kisosen snapped his head toward the sound to see Mali humma rising quickly from a consultation with Chief Yanegwa in front of the Council House, arms thrown out in disgust. "These plans are short-sighted and foolish!" he shouted, his eyebrows pinched tightly together and upper lip curled into a sneer. "I have seen with my own eyes what happens when you welcome the white man! They disguise their evil with "gifts" that promise a better life, but in the end they bring nothing but pain and suffering. This plan will lead us to doom!"

Chief Yanegwa spoke some words in return, but they were not audible to those seated in the center of the plaza. Mali humma spun and stomped away, then after a few steps wretched himself back around with an expression of loathing set on his angular face. "I've had enough! Tanampi and I will not accompany you tomorrow to the council. You can find someone else to be your muscle! We go on the hunt!" He motioned wildly to the north. "We'll do something useful like slaying that bear who is digging at the crops in the north field. We'll return in glory with fresh meat and a warm skin to celebrate Shotek's marriage next month."

The entire tribe watched as Mali humma stormed off toward his family hut, trailed by his brother Tanampi. Shotek's thick eyelids looked surprised at the announcement, and he squirmed uncomfortably. He then slinked off after his father and uncle to see if he would be allowed to join this hunt that was unexpectedly for the purpose of welcoming his own bride.

After several beats of pregnant silence, murmurs darted through the tribe as they swapped feelings about the hostile exchange.

"Shameful! If he were a real father, he would let Shotek fell the bear for his own bride. Shameful!" An unidentified women behind Kisosen chided. "Mali humma is always threatening to leave and join the southern tribe. I just wish he would go and do it!"

Another woman hissed back in reply. "I grow tired of his complaining!"

"Father," Hialeah appeared deftly in front of Kisosen gathering his hand in hers, "why don't you lay down and take a nap in the hut? You look so worn through."

Kisosen breathed in and out once before replying. "No, but thank you." He rose to his feet, both knees popping in protest. "I must be more useful than that. Leotie said there were ripe blueberries in the north woods. I will take a basket and see what I can find." He looked down at her worried face. "Fret not, child. I will be fine."

The solid meal and slow walk to the north meadow cleared Kisosen's head. Darkening clouds scuttled across the sky blocking Hashi's afternoon heat. It didn't yet smell of rain, but the sky definitely signaled its approach.

He swung the basket lazily between two fingers of his right hand, finally pushing it into a cheery clump of light pink flowering Rosebay rhododendrons that rimmed the edge of the meadow. As it had already started to cool before he left the village after lunch, he had grabbed his deerskin cloak from the family hut and thrown it over his shoulders. He absent-mindedly caressed the rose-shaped head of the carved bone pin that secured the cloak at his neckline. It was a gift he had made for his wife many years ago. He should have buried it along with the rest of her possessions at her burial, but he could not stand to part with it. It was her favorite pin and she wore it faithfully over her heart every day. At the risk of bringing bad omens, he kept it with him always.

He waded into the deep grasses of the meadow which reached near to his hips. Pulling the cloak tightly around him, he wriggled down into the deep, cool grass, found a comfortable spot to rest his head, and immediately fell into a deep and trouble-free sleep.

Chapter 4

It was sometime later when Kisosen awoke in a daze to a murmur of voices. Sleep pulled at him beckoning his return, but the voices grew louder and roused him to full consciousness. He lay motionless -- frozen so as not to give away his presence. It would be embarrassing to be caught napping when he should be working. At first, he could not make out the words spoken or even the timbre of the voices, but gradually they moved closer and it became alarmingly clear who had just joined him in the meadow.

"I'm not sure," the harsh, but subdued voice of Tanampi washed over Kisosen. "I agree that Yanegwa is wrong, but it seems so drastic. What if something goes wrong? What if we are caught?"

"The words of a coward! Are you my brother or my sister?" hissed the distinct and unmistakable voice of Mali humma. "Yanegwa must be dealt with! This is the only way."

A long pause... followed only by sounds of feet swishing through and stamping on grass. The pair stopped suddenly only feet from Kisosen. Mali humma's low, but jarring words sliced through

Kisosen's head like he spat them directly into his ear. "He must die - and you know it."

A disgruntled and hesitant grunt from Tanampi, followed by silence. "But... why kill the entire traveling party?" more grunting and stamping. "Could we not use that arrow from the Catawba? Hide in that massive oak on the southern trail. Strike only at Yanegwa from the hidden branches of the tree. Fell him and then run like the wind..."

"Hide like cowards and strike in secrecy!?!" interrupted Mali humma. "What kind of honor kill is that!!!"

"Not an honor kill," hissed Tanampi. "But - very much like the sniveling Catawba! It would be convincing!"

A resigned grunt, followed by the sounds of one man taking a few steps, thankfully, in a direction away from where Kisosen lay frozen holding his breath. Several minutes dragged by with only the sounds of shifting and breathing. Kisosen dared a few shallow breaths himself.

"Alright," that sounded like Mali humma. "We'll kill the bear as it returns from the Great River this evening. Before Hashi's awakening, we circle wide to the east and make our way to the Great Oak that stands guarding the southern mountain pass. We strike the death blow - at Yanegwa only - and fly like the wind back over the eastern ridge. We can be back here to the north woods by the time Hashi is half past high in the sky. Then we skin the bear and carry as much of the carcass as we can back to the village through the north gate arriving at the evening meal to songs and wails of lament." Mali humma's voice had turned sour and mocking at the end.

An uncertain grunt from Tanampi. "The time will be tight. Maybe I should tend to the bear, while you tend to Yanegwa."

"No!" barked Mali humma followed by the sound of pushing and grabbing. "We do this together. If one of us fails, the other must finish!"

A long, resigned sigh escaped from Tanampi. "All right brother. We do it your way." The sound of grass swishing resumed. Kisosen strained to catch their continued conversation as the two moved away into the trees. "I just hope you've thought this through..."

Kisosen lay unmoving for what seemed an eternity. A jumble of thoughts and anxieties crashed and tumbled through his head. 'What should he do? He must warn Chief Yanegwa. But how?' He turned the options over and over in his mind, but none seemed right. Finally, he wrestled himself to his feet, stiff from laying so long in one position. 'What a disaster! He came seeking sleep and an escape from his problems, and now he had only a greater burden to shoulder!'

He glanced up at the sky and realized with alarm that the evening meal was soon at hand. Moving faster than he had since the death of his wife more than a year ago, he hurried through the woods and down the north path back to the village.

Chapter 5

The meal that evening was a celebration honoring the next day's journey of Chief Yanegwa and a small traveling party to a regional council of the seven local tribes. The situation with the white settlers was a growing concern. A messenger had visited the village several weeks ago with notification of a council meeting to take place two days after the next full moon.

Chaska and his hunting party had returned laden with freshly caught river trout and rabbit which now lay sizzling over the coals of several fires. There was freshly roasted corn on the cob, the boiled starchy seeds and spinach-like greens of newly harvested chenopodium, berries, nuts, acorns, and roasted wild potatoes and zamia roots. Sassafrass tea complimented the din of the villagers' chatter that rose like a bubble of contentment over the central plaza.

Chief Yanegwa was seated at his bench of honor surrounded by the elders of the tribe. His long, intricately carved, ceremonial tobacco pipe perched ready at his feet to seal the internal agreement of items to be brought from the tribe and discussed at the council meeting. Perhaps the chief also intended to offer the pipe to Mali humma in a ritual designed to end their hostilities.

Kisosen, too distracted by his thoughts to participate in the ritual ceremony, moved from the eastern benches and settled on the west side of the plaza with the younger women and children. They buzzed and chatted with excitement at the activity of the celebration.

Ahyoka, looking up in surprise, finally noticed her grandfather sitting there just outside the edge of the circle. She rushed forward and threw herself down beside him, leaning heavily on his arm. "Kisosen! We have an important question to ask you about Hashi." Her high, clear voice cut across the individual conversations of the other women and children in the circle. Stories of Hashi were important. And questions usually led to stories.

Another child named Shikoba quickly picked up where Ahyoka left off. "Yes, yes, we have a question! Please, please may I ask it?" His small, dark eyes peered up optimistically at Kisosen -- his hands clasped together tightly under his chin. "Please?"

Kisosen blew out a tired breath. He needed to set out for the mountain. He needed to think and decide what to do. He looked around at all the hopeful faces of the women and children. 'Well,' he thought, 'this problem will definitely wait.'

"My dear Shikoba, what is it that you want to know?"

"Oh, Great Kisosen! Thank you!" said Shikoba in a thankful rush of breath. "My question is..." he paused to let the anticipation build, "why does Hashi go to bed over there," pointing his small hand over the river to the west, "but when she gets up in the morning, she is over there?" swinging his arm in a full half circle to point to the east. A twitter of approval ran through the remaining children in the circle as many started hopping up and down and clapping in delight. Many of the mothers exchanged knowing glances. This was a favorite question and a well-told story.

Kisosen pushed his anxieties away and settled down to enjoy the telling of the story. "Well, Shikoba. Have you ever gone to sleep on one side of your mat, only to find that when you awoke, you were on the other side?"

Shikoba tilted his head looking up to the sky and placed his right index finger next to his mouth as he carefully considered the question. Most of the other children were already nodding their heads vigorously in agreement. "I guess so..." Shikoba replied in a hesitant tone.

"Well, that happens when you don't sleep very well. When you are restless, or worried, or very, very tired." Kisosen donned a serious expression looking attentively at the small child.

"I see," Shikoba replied.

"You see," Kisosen continued, "Hashi has many responsibilities to tend to each day. She must bring us light so that we can see where we are going and don't bump into things." The children giggled as Kisosen continued. "She must bring us heat so that the water does not freeze and the rain does not turn to snow. She must also bring nourishment to all of the trees, and the corn, and the plants so they can grow deep, strong roots and healthy, towering stalks - which they need to feed us and all the other animals of the land." A collective sigh of acknowledgment ran through the group.

"Not only does Hashi carry a great basket of responsibilities on her back," Kisosen looked up toward the sky where Hashi was now playing peek-a-boo behind the scurry of moving clouds, "but she is very restless. Do you see how quickly she moves across the sky each day?" Kisosen paused to let the children consider the question. When he began to see a chorus of nods, he continued. "She never stops moving. She never really rests. So, when she sleeps she rolls over and over and travels the width of her mat. But, while your mat is only this wide," Kisosen moved his hands until the palms were facing and they were about two feet apart, "Hashi's is as wide as the land is long." He then spread his arms as wide as they would go. The children collectively gasped in awe, stunned at the thought of a cornhusk mat stretching as far as they could see.

"That's why she is so angry and hot at mid-day," Kisosen concluded. "She is tired and cranky from not sleeping well. She needs a nap, but will not take one. That's why we have to put her to bed at night. She does not want to go. Then she is too tired in the morning to wake up by herself." He rocked back on his tailbone and rested his hands on his hips. "So, now, I need you all to set a good example for Hashi and show her how to go to bed nicely."

Kisosen rose slowly to his feet as the children crowded forward to give him a good night hug and thank him for the story. "I think that Hashi will be especially cranky tonight after playing tag with the rain clouds for most of the day. I must go now and tend to her." He gave as many of the children as he could reach a collective squeeze. "Be good now, and show her how it is done."

Chapter 6

The journey that evening back to the top of Tanawha Mountain was one of the most difficult Kisosen could remember. Just as he reached the edge of the tribe's southern field lightning began streaking across the western sky and rumbles of thunder announced the rapid approach of the storm. Halfway up the mountain, the clouds burst open, dumping a rush of water like a bucket suddenly tipped over by a clumsy giant.

Kisosen pushed into his mountain-top hut wetter than if he had jumped into the river. With the rainwater puddling around him, he clumsily built a fire taking multiple strikes with his flint to create a spark big enough to enflame an awaiting tuft of animal fur. Moving quickly he carefully nurtured the small flame until a blaze was securely crackling in the central hearth of the hut.

He glanced out at the blackening western sky now completely obscured with angry, fast-moving clouds. Hashi was nowhere to be seen. What was the point of putting her to bed when he had no idea if she was even attending? He paused unmoving, frozen with indecision, then threw up his hands.

What difference did it make? He was already as wet as he was going to be.

Exiting the hut, he moved carefully to the western side of the mountain top plaza built centuries ago by his ancestors. He raised his arms and planted his feet. The rain pelted his upturned face. His brain was empty, though. No words came to mind. After a few minutes the rain suddenly softened and turned to a steady drizzle. A dull and quiet clap of thunder hunkered in the distance. He stood unmoving... unthinking.

"Hashi," the words suddenly tumbled from him. "Please guide me. I beseech you. Show me the way!" Tears and raindrops mingled together splashing down his lined and weathered face. "Show me how to save the chief. Show me how to teach Mali humma humility and grace. Show me this, and I will never doubt you or my purpose again. I will be your humble servant until my last breath!" With that, Kisosen fell to his knees letting the rain wash away his worries and anxieties. "Give me peace..."

Chapter 7

The rain had stopped. The mountain stood solidly, dark, dripping. Kisosen could hear the individual raindrops first joining in pairs, which then joined other pairs into quartets, which then joined into octets. The octets then melded into tiny rivulets all racing down the sides of Tanawha Mountain toward the now swollen and rushing Great River. He lay with his eyes closed, a weariness so deep, so chasmic, there was no bottom. He could not sleep, but he was not awake either. He pictured Hashi restlessly tossing and turning in her bed. He had only heard Mali humma and Tanampi's evil plotting in the meadow, but Hashi had seen it. While the clouds may have partially obscured her view, she was wise enough to recognize treachery when she saw it.

"Of course!" Kisosen spoke aloud sitting bolt upright on his mat. "Hashi SAW it!" He folded his legs under and awkwardly pushed himself to a shaky stand. "She saw it! And now she has told me what to do!"

Kisosen hastily pulled on his long deerskin trousers and tunic that had been drying on a rack on the other side of the fire. He fumbled with his belt, but finally managed a secure knot. Tossing his cloak over his shoulders, he fastened it securely with his wife's rose pin. He gathered his bow, dart gun, and quiver of arrows slinging each over his head and across his shoulders. Fumbling for his knife, he drove it decidedly into the sheath hanging from the right side of his belt. He also had blow darts in a pouch hanging from his belt should he need them. Without even banking the fire, he darted from the hut and hit the trail back to the village at a reckless pace.

By now the storm had passed and the sky was clear. The moon, almost full, reflected its light bouncing between the standing puddles and glistening leaves. Deep shadows of inky black hung menacingly under trees, boulders, and shrubs. He must take care not to run into any wolves or the cougars that hunted the mountains and valleys at night. Traveling the three miles between the mountain top and the village was a dangerous venture at night.

The trail was slippery with mud causing Kisosen to stumble and slide. The moon, being almost full, was directly overhead at its highest point in the sky. When the path wound around a boulder on either side, though, the trail was plunged into almost full darkness. At this first dark stretch, his rash pace caused him to trip fully over a good-sized rock that the gushing rain had washed onto the trail. Chiding himself bitterly for not thinking to bring a torch, he picked himself up rubbing both his left hand and knee. He had ripped open his trouser at the knee and could feel blood trickling down his leg. 'No matter,' he thought thrusting away the pain, 'what will happened to Chief Yanegwa is much worse than a skinned knee.'

After this first fall, Kisosen moderated his pace each time the path fell into darkness. With these delays it took nearly twice as long to complete the climb down Tanawha Mountain. When he finally hit the more level track at the edge of the valley, his knee and hand were throbbing acutely in perfect sync with his pounding heart.

Picking up his pace to a stiff trot, he hurried down the slowly descending track. One mile down, two to go. Unaccustomed to vigorous exercise at his advancing age, his breath quickly became heavy and labored. "Please Hashi," he wheezed, "keep the wolves at bay. My task is so much more important than to be a meal for the pack."

Just as the tops of the cornstalks at the edge of the south tribal field came into view, he heard the distance yelping cry of a lone grey wolf. Terror flooded over him as he spun on the spot trying to identify the direction of the sound. Another undulating howl answered the first from a different direction. He fought down his panic. 'They are not that close. If I run now, I can beat them to the palisade!'

Adrenaline flooded his veins as he turned and began running full out toward the village. His breath now came in ragged gasps. He knew there were men in the fields guarding the crops who might be close enough to come to his aid if he called, but he felt it was important to keep this midnight visit a secret if at all possible.

Twinkles of white light flashed in his vision and his lungs felt near to bursting when the pointed tips of the village palisade floated into sight. He quickly lunged toward the gate scrabbling his hands over each log moving to the left, desperate to find the larger anchor post that marked the outermost edge of the gate.

"There!" he gasped with relief. Gathering his wits and fighting a rising panic as another chorus of howls and yips echoed behind him - much closer now - he began moving to the left, quickly counting each log. At a count of 25, he dropped to the ground pawing the soil. When he painfully stubbed his right fingers on the rock he was feeling for, he clawed at its edges until he was able to lift it from its bed.

Another series of howls! His breath was shallow and rapid as he stole a quick glance over his shoulder, imagining the beady yellow eyes of the wolf pack advancing on his position. He had the rope in his hands. A quick yank and he heard the click of the latch releasing inside the hidden gate. He pushed roughly on the logs and the gate swung easily inward. Launching himself through the gate, he slammed it quickly behind leaning heavily on the rough logs. The latch closed with a click and he fell to the ground in relief.

Chapter 8

Kisosen sat on the ground for nearly five minutes, just breathing. 'In and out,' he told himself with each breath. 'Just settle yourself. You made it.' He glanced up at the sky. The moon was a great, orange-grey ball suspended on a sea of black. Its position in the sky told him that he now had less than four hours before he had to awaken Hashi. He pushed that problem aside. "One step at a time!" he muttered, if only just to reassure himself.

He pushed himself to a wobbly stand. His left knee was throbbing. The other was trembling. Both hands shook. His back ached. He thrust one foot forward, willing himself to creep quietly toward the Council House.

At the door of the Council House, Kisosen carefully pushed back the animal skin. Crouching, he called softly, "Chief Yanegwa. Chief! It is Kisosen. I must speak to you." He froze, listening intently. A soft rustle of skins and bodies signaled that someone was aware of his presence. "Chief Yanegwa!" Kisosen projected his whisper into the depths of the hut. "It's Kisosen."

A broad, round, weathered face suddenly loomed in front of him. He drew back in surprise. "This must be important, to bring you to me in the middle of the night," the chief returned his whisper.

"It is," breathed Kisosen. "It is the most urgent matter you can imagine." Kisosen fell silent struggling to find the beginning of his tale. "I must speak to you. But, what I say must not be heard by others."

"Then," Chief Yanegwa whispered in reply, "let us go to south gate away from the huts and where we can see all around us."

The two elders ducked out through the hanging buckskin and moved silently through the night toward the gate. Once there, they huddled together. The chief caught Kisosen's eye with an expectant gaze. "What is it, good friend? What could make you risk a most perilous trip down the mountain on a night such as this?"

"I... I..." Kisosen stammered.

Chief Yanegwa placed a reassuring hand on his arm. "Just speak the truth, and all will be well."

Kisosen drew in a sharp breath. 'Well,' he thought, 'this won't be exactly the truth....'

"Chief, my friend. You know I deeply respect and admire you. Even as we played on the riverbank as boys, I respected you then."

Chief Yanegwa chuckled softly, clearly lost in the memory of those earlier days. The two were close to the same age, growing up as devoted and inseparable childhood friends. They hunted together as young men, felling their first black bear together. "Just tell me Itanale," breathed Yanegwa using the name given to Kisosen by his maternal grandmother.

"You are in great danger my friend," the words tumbled from Kisosen's lips. A stabbing pain shot through Kisosen's lower back causing him to straighten and let out a small grunt.

"What do you mean?" replied the chief.

"Hashi... Hashi told me a frightening 'bedtime' story." Kisosen averted his eyes to keep the chief from seeing the lie. "Hashi does not speak to me often. When she does... well, she speaks the truth. You must believe her! You must listen!" Kisosen's voice took on an urgent tone raising in both pitch and volume.

Chief Yanegwa made a shushing motion with his hands. "I will listen. I will believe. If Hashi told you -- then it must be so."

"Hashi has seen the future. She says... if you go to the regional council tomorrow, you will... you will die."

The chief drew in a slow breath. Kisosen noticed, as if for the first time, the chief's high cheekbones, his strong forehead and angular chin... his wide, slightly downturned mouth, and lined and weathered face. The chief took a few steps away, hands on hips, and looked up to the moon, as if for guidance. After nearly a minute, he retraced his steps to retake his place close to Kisosen.

"Do you have more details? How would this occur?" The chief's heavy eyelids were narrowed in fierce concentration.

Kisosen shook his head. "Hashi was... when Hashi speaks... it is often in proverbs." Kisosen stopped to collect his thoughts. 'Should he tell the chief about Mali humma? What would the chief do if he knew? Would he actually believe that Hashi overheard Mali humma and Tanampi's conversation? Hashi was great and powerful, but could she really be listening in on every conversation in this great valley on any given day?'

Kisosen looked up to find the chief staring at him. Their dark eyes locked in a penetrating gaze. "Hashi was vague about the details, but very clear about the result. If you go, you will die," Kisosen said, slowly drawing out those last words.

Moments slipped away while the two hunkered together in silence. "What are you going to do?" whispered Kisosen.

"Hmmm," Yanegwa grunted. "I will have to meditate." He turned and looked up, scrutinizing the moon. "It is late. You must return to the mountain to awaken Hashi."

A look of panic flashed over Kisosen's face as he thought of another hazardous journey back to the mountain top, pursued by wolves.

"Dear friend," Yanegwa reached out and clutched his arm in reassurance, "awaken Chaska to go with you. You mustn't chance the wolves again in your return. Chaska should begin to learn your ways. He can stand with you to keep any wolves at bay, and then help you in the morning with Hashi."

Kisosen smiled weakly in return. "Thank you dear friend. I will do that." He gripped Chief Yanegwa's arm with a returning squeeze. "Now, go. Begin your meditation. You have a very important decision to make."

Kisosen watched the chief return to the Council House, clearly lost in deep thought. He turned toward his family hut to awaken Chaska, but then stopped. 'If Chaska comes with me,' he thought, 'we will have to go all the way back to the mountain top. Twelve miles in one night is too much. I will, instead, go only to the high stand of rocks just past the southern field. Atop these I will be safe from wolves and can still awaken Hashi.'

With the decision made, he set out limping toward the hidden gate.

Chapter 9

Mali humma and Tanampi's night had not gone well. To speed the hunt they had caught a beaver earlier in the day and hung the carcass from a marking tree along the bear's regular trail. Below the beaver carcass, they had left a pile of rotting fish. Each had chosen a separate tree about 30 feet downwind on either side of the bait. Settling into a sturdy crook of branches about ten feet off the ground, they waited with arrows already nocked.

In spite of the powerful stink of the bait, the wait was long. The hope had been to make the kill by late afternoon, leaving the remainder of the evening to gut, skin, and debone the bear. They had brought buckskins to wrap the meat and bones in, planning to weigh the bundles down in the cool, deeper waters of the Great River. This would keep the meat and bones fresher to convince the tribe that the bear had been killed the next morning.

As the afternoon wore on and the shadows started to deepen under the trees, Mali humma grew impatient. He tried to occupy himself by visualizing and rehearsing each step of the plan, but as the day grew later and later, this only served to heighten his irritation and anxiety. It was well within an hour of Hashi-sleep before the bear came lumbering lazily along the trail from the direction of the river.

Due to Mali humma's amplified impatience, he rashly drew his bow long before the bear had settled into the bait. When the time finally came to release the arrow, his back and shoulder muscles were already quivering with fatigue. The goal was to place the shot immediately behind the front shoulder, a location that allowed easy penetration into the vital organs, killing the animal quickly. Of the two brothers, Mali humma had the best shot as the bear had settled on his side of the marking tree.

He sighted and let his arrow fly.

The shot was high and sliced harmlessly over the bear's shoulders, thudding noisily into the marking tree. The bear reared onto back legs letting out a startled roar and took off with great speed along the trail. Fortunately, Tanampi had already drawn his bow and let loose an arrow directly in front of the bear's path. The bear ran into the arrow and it plunged deeply into its side. Unfortunately, the arrow missed the bear's heart and after an initial stumble, it shot off through the trees.

Tanampi and Mali humma, fuming at his miss, jumped stiffly down from their perches and began to follow the bear, its trail easily marked with splatters of blood. Within seconds of their departure, though, a loud clap of thunder announced the arrival of the storm, and the heavens let loose with a torrent of showers.

Cursing loudly over their bad luck, Mali humma took off at a run to find the bear before the blood trail was washed away. Tanampi yelled after him, "Brother, be careful! A wounded animal is dangerous!"

Tanampi's words died unregistered in Mali humma's ears as he rushed rashly after his prey. The storm plunged the forest into near darkness, and in Mali humma's haste, he literally stumbled over the bear which was now staggering with its last steps. The angry and frightened animal turned on Mali humma, landing a fierce swipe of its long and deadly claws across its pursuer's chest. Mali humma was thrown back against a tree.

Before the bear could fall on Mali humma, though, Tanampi muscular body shot out of the darkness, leaping over his brother's prostrate form, and plunged his knife deep into the bear throat. The bear seized Tanampi in a final death hug, then the two fell together, thudding awkwardly to the ground. As Tanampi rolled free, the bear gave a final shudder and drew its last breath.

The two brothers lay gasping and bleeding on the now soggy, leaf-strewn forest floor. The earthy scent produced when rain falls on dry soil, mixed with the smell of ozone, wafted past them. The trees thrashed angrily in the rushing winds of the storm.

Mali humma rolled onto his back, face to the sky, the deluge of rain washing into his wound. He was startled by the strong grasp of his brother's hand on his shoulder. "Are you okay?"

"Yes," Mali humma replied fingering the injury on his chest. "It's only a scratch. How about you?"

Tanampi grunted in reply and reached out a hand to help Mali humma to his feet. "You were lucky. That was extremely stupid!"

Mali humma, now in a shaky stand, kicked the bear in frustration and turned in a full circle to take in their situation. "Well, stupid or not, at least we have the bear. Let's get on with it."

Chapter 10

It rained for hours. The dark of the night fell upon the two brothers rapidly. The storm clouds completely obscured the moon. With no light and no ability to start a fire, the two had few options. Tanampi decided to attempt a crude gutting of the bear in the near blackness of the forest.

The two brothers rolled the bear unto its back and tied each leg to a separate tree to expose its belly. Tanampi felt between the back legs until he located the bear's anus. Using his knife, he cut around the anus until the anal tract was free. Mali humma then held the end of the anal tract closed to keep the feces and urine from polluting the abdominal cavity.

Tanampi carefully cut an incision from pelvis to sternum, excising the skin and abdominal wall. He tried not to puncture the intestines, but in the dark he could not be sure he had not fouled the abdomen. Reaching into the slimy cavity, he located the bear's stomach by feel. With knife tucked in hand, he followed the esophagus as high up into the chest cavity as he could, and cut through the bear's esophagus and windpipe. With the two ends of the intestinal tract now free, he yanked out the windpipe, lungs, heart, intestines, organs, and anal tract, depositing the slimy mass onto the forest floor.

The two brothers stood in the rain for several minutes arguing next steps. After the chase, they were now too far away to drag the 200 pound carcass through the mud back to the river. While they could probably skin the bear in the dark, the job would be crude. A bad skinning job would not support the story that they had killed the bear in the morning and taken the day to skin and dress the carcass. Without skinning the bear first, it was not possible to dismember and split the carcass into smaller pieces which could be strapped to their backs for easier carrying. And without a fire to keep wolves and scavengers at bay, it was much too dangerous to stay by the carcass for the night. After much debate, the brothers settled on hanging the gutted carcass from the nearest tree.

In the dark, it was not possible to throw their ropes over a branch. While Tanampi tied one end of a rope to each of the bear's back legs, Mali humma tied good-sized rocks to the other ends. Securing the rock-end of the ropes around his waist, he climbed the nearest tree by feel and located a sturdy branch. Throwing the rocks over the branch, the two brothers then hauled the bear carcass high into the tree.

With the bear carcass safely stashed, they did their best to note their position in the forest, and

then started slogging their way through the mud and
rain toward the eastern ridge where they had
planned to spend the night.

Chapter 11

The dawn of the next morning arrived in a brilliant splash of natural color. The lingering water droplets in the air from the previous night's storm intensified Hashi's flamboyant entrance to the day. The gentleness of the morning air, vibrating with the song of crickets and birds, was incongruous with the vile betrayal planned for just a few hours later.

The village stirred just as it did every morning -- women starting fires and grinding corn to make sofkee; children greeting friends and bringing water from the river for their mothers; men preparing weapons for the hunt or tools for the field.

Amid the morning bustle, Chief Yanegwa sat cross-legged, with palms upturned resting on his knees, in soundless meditation by the fire in the Council House. Ghigau knew not to disturb him. As the members of the traveling party approached the hut to make final preparations for the journey, she turned each away motioning silently that they must wait.

The beauty and calmness of the morning gradually melted into growing tension as each tribe member became aware that a change in plans was eminent. Chaska and Hialeah, distracted by the uncertainty of Chief Yanegwa's sudden and unexplained meditation, did not notice that Kisosen had failed to return to the village even though it was well past an hour after Hashi-wake.

Finally the chief rose stiffly from his meditative pose, stretched, and slowly ducked through the door of the Council House. Blinking in the bright light, he greeted the gathering crowd of men milling about the central plaza awaiting his direction.

"Friends, I am sorry to keep you waiting," Chief Yanegwa croaked due to the dryness of his mouth. He cleared his throat and motioned to his wife to bring some water. "I have received an edict from Hashi. She has decreed that I not go to the Council meeting," he rasped over a loud murmur that traveled through the tribe.

"But, we must go!" Chaska stepped forward stating what many other were thinking. "There are important issues to discuss. The white settlers...!"

"Yes... and we will go," Yanegwa breathed out slowly. "I will send a proxy in my place."

A startled buzz passed through the group gathered in the plaza. 'Who could possibly be Chief Yanegwa's proxy? Who would he choose?'

"Shotek," Yanegwa called out more strongly now. "Bring me Shotek."

Amid a susurrous murmur, Shotek, who had been lurking at the edge of the crowd, was pushed to the front to now stand shakily in front of Chief Yanegwa. The young man's almond-shaped eyes darted nervously as he wiped his drippy, hook-shaped nose with the back on one hand.

"Shotek," the chief moved forward, firmly gripping the upper arms of the sweating youth. "When I look into your heart, I see that you are brave and wise. You will be my proxy and go in my place."

Chief Yanegwa's statement was quickly followed by a chorus of shocked and disgruntled cries from the other men in the tribe. He raised his voice to be heard over the growing protests. "I believe you will represent the tribe well. I am confident you will carry our message truthfully to the council."

Shotek struggled to gain control of his deeply tanned face, snapping shut his gaping jaw. "Tha... thank you..." he stammered. "I will... do my best to... to honor you and... and represent the proud heritage of... of our tribe."

"Remember the tribal pact we agreed on last night," the chief said giving Shotek's shoulders an assuring squeeze. "Pass on our messages to the council, and you will do well."

Shotek nodded. "I am honored that you have chosen me as your proxy," he said hesitantly looking down at the chief's feet. "But, how will they know that I am truly authorized to speak for you? I am a young warrior... unknown to most on the Council."

Chief Yanegwa looked up at Hashi as if asking for her advice. He then looked around at the men and women clustered around them. "I will give you my turkey feather cape and my ceremonial hair roach."

The chief unfastened the short, colorful turkey feather cape he wore as a symbol of his position, and swung it decidedly over Shotek's shoulders. He thrust the carved bone pin through the four holes to fastened it securely under Shotek's chin.

"Bring me my ceremonial hair roach!" the chief called.

Ghigau broke herself from her shocked stance, and stumbled into the Council House to retrieve the red, white, black, and yellow hair roach made from the stiff guard hair of a porcupine, white tail hair of the deer, and the black beard of the turkey -- the roach Chief Yanegwa always wore at ceremonies and while traveling to meetings or visits with other villages. Upon her return, she and Shotek's mother removed his daily hair roach and fitted the chief's onto Shotek's shiny black hair. Shotek shook his head from side to side feeling the majestic weight of the long roach that reached half way down his bare back.

While the roach was attached, Chief Yanegwa organized the remainder of the party. "Where is Kisosen?" the chief questioned, searching the faces of the men in the plaza.

Chaska looked around in alarm, "I do not know." With swiftly growing anxiety, he asked urgently, "Has anyone seen him?" A chorus of negative responses swept through the crowd. Chaska darted off to his family hut to see if Kisosen was there.

He was back in a flash, his face lined with worry. "Hialeah says he has not come for his breakfast. We have not seen him since he left for the mountain last night."

A resolute expression settled on Chief Yanegwa's face. He raised his arms to calm the tribe. "It is late. The traveling party must go. Chaska, you will go and tend to your father. Onsi, Malili, Losa, you will accompany Shotek in the traveling party."

He reached out to each man in turn placing his hand upon each head. "Go in peace. May Hashi's strength and wisdom carry you through this journey of great consequence."

The last to receive his blessing was Shotek. Chief Yanegwa held his hand on Shotek's head at length, eye's closed, mumbling inaudible prayers and blessings. Opening his eyes he met Shotek's gaze and offered a traditional traveling prayer.

> *O Great Hashi,*
> *Help this brave warrior*
> *to always speak the truth quietly,*
> *To listen with an open mind*
> *when others speak,*

*To remember the peace
that may be found in silence.*

With that, the chief turned slowly on his heel
and shuffled tiredly back to the Council House where
he collapsed onto his mat, falling instantly into a
deep and trouble-free sleep.

Chapter 12

When Hashi's first light seeped over the edge of the rocky outcrop where Mali humma and Tanampi had sought shelter a few hours before, it found them both prostrate and in a state of extreme exhaustion. Mali humma groaned softly, stretching his stiff and sore torso, and shook Tanampi's broad, muscular shoulder to wake him. "Brother, we must go. It is still several hours walk to the Great Oak."

Tanampi rolled over and grumbled in annoyance. He rubbed his hands vigorously over his broad, round copper-colored face and massaged his sleep-heavy eyelids. Like his brother, he had a low hairline capping the top of a strong forehead, and an angular chin that gave him a heroic, noble look. "I'm not leaving until I eat. You can stumble your way to 'greatness' afflicted with hunger, but I choose not to."

With a grunt of resigned agreement, the two brothers reached into their knapsacks and drew out a portion of the dried berries, nuts, and pemmican they carried for their journey.

While they ate, Tanampi examined the wound on Mali humma's chest. The four gashes were not deep, but gaped open, now fiery red, swollen, and edged with dried blood. "The poison is coming to this wound. Along the way, we must look for herbs to make a poultice to draw out the heat."

"There is no need!" replied Mali humma gruffly. "It's not bad. A small sacrifice for a much greater gain."

The two brother's trek to the Great Oak was uneventful, interrupted only by a short stop at a tarn to drink, fill their water skins, and wash the mud and filth from their bodies and clothing. Mali humma brooded, turning the plan over and over in his mind... agonizing over the fact that the meat of the bear carcass would probably foul in the heat of the day. Maybe they should just skin the bear and leave the carcass for the wolves. His wound was getting worse. By nightfall the poison would be fully upon him. They could claim the injury prevented them from saving the carcass -- that wolves came upon them while they were skinning -- that they were unable to fight them off. That had happened before. It was believable. Besides, he thought, with the villagers deep in mourning over the death of their chief, no one would notice or dwell on the inconsistencies in their story.

A grunt from Tanampi interrupted Mali humma's ruminations. "There is the oak," he said pointing to the great tree near the top of a rise. "I've been thinking." Tanampi turned to face his brother. "We should not both be in that tree."

"It's too late for second thoughts, brother!" Mali humma countered testily, his face pinched in anger.

Tanampi stopped short and roared back in reply. "And your hatred clouds your judgment, 'brother'!" He waved his long arm in the direction of the trail which passed directly under the tree.

"If we are both in the oak, we will not see the party approaching. The path rises sharply coming out of the woods. You need to let the arrow fly as soon as Yanegwa hits the top of the rise. If he's any closer, we will not be able to outrun Malili. He is due to be in the party. He is the fastest runner in the village!"

Tanampi spun his long, lean body to face his brother and thrust his broad face so close to Mali humma's that their hooked noses almost touched. "Your hatred makes your mind weak!" Tanampi spat. "When you are ruled by Vengeance, you usually lose!"

Tanampi stomped away, then turned back abruptly. "I will be in that chestnut over there," he said, pointing to a tree nearer the top of the rise, but still a distance from the trail. "When I see them come out of the woods, I will sound the call of the hawk." He threw back his dark head and cupped both hands in front of his mouth, demonstrating the cry of a Cooper's Hawk.

"When you hear that sound, ready your arrow." Tanampi strode decidedly away toward the Chestnut tree, then turned back once more. "And brother, push Vengeance aside. **He** is a bad shot."

Chapter 13

Chaska, worried for his father's safety, quickly returned to the family hut to gather his weapons.

"Where are you going?" asked Hialeah.

"I'm going to find Father."

"But," Hialeah countered, "what of the traveling party? It is late. They surely can't wait."

"I'm not going this time." Chaska darted from the hut with Hialeah and Ahyoka in tow. "I will find Father and bring him home." As he trotted away toward the south gate, Chaska called over his shoulder, worry evident in his voice, "Have something ready for Father to eat."

Chaska covered the three miles to the mountain top in speedy time. He considered stopping to search clumps of bushes along the trail, but decided he could do that, if needed, on the way back. He felt certain that Kisosen was somewhere on Tanawha Mountain, either on the steep and rocky trail or still on the mountain top. His fears heightened further when he hit the steepest part of the trail and started to see spatters of dried blood on the rocks.

When Chaska emerged at the top of Tanawha Mountain, all was eerily quiet except the keening of the wind. Hashi's light filtered down gently through scattered clouds, tossing darting shadows across the pebble-covered plaza.

"Father!" Chaska called. Receiving no answer but the whistling of wind, he darted inside the hut throwing back the buckskin. The fire was out. The hut was empty. A quick darting glance told Chaska that at least Kisosen was armed. He always carried a knife, bow, and blowgun, and all were missing.

Chaska walked to the east edge of the plaza and stared up a Hashi. "Where is he?" he implored.

Hashi remained silent, choosing only to return his stare. "Tell me your secrets, Great Hashi."

Chaska planted his feet and raised his arms, trying to find the position his father described in his salute to Hashi. He closed his eyes and focused his mind, feeling the warmth of Hashi's light on his face and the wind playfully lifting his hair. He envisioned himself as the Kisosen. A sense of peace crept over him. A prayer his father had taught him floated into his mind, and he whispered it aloud.

> *O Great Hashi,*
> *Make me wise, so that I understand,*
> *The things you have taught my people.*
> *Let me learn the lesson you have hidden*
> *In every leaf and rock.*

I seek strength,
Not to be greater than my brother.
But to fight against my greatest enemy -
Myself.

Chaska stood frozen waiting to see if Hashi would speak. The minutes stretched by. His arms grew tired and his shoulder muscles began to quiver. He finally opened his eyes and let his arms drop to his side, letting out a sigh of relief. Hashi had moved noticeably in the sky.

"Thank you, Great Hashi," Chaska whispered.

Chapter 14

The four men that left the village that morning bound for the regional council meeting walked the first five miles in stunned silence, each man wrestling with his own reaction to Chief Yanegwa's seemingly irrational decision. While they plodded on, Hashi cast a watchful eye on the party's progress. So consumed with their own ruminations, they failed to notice the thousands of painted blossoms now covering the valley and forest floor. Flowering trillium, lady slippers, japonicas, jack-in-the-pulpits, wild ginger, evening primrose, and mountain laurel all bowed in the tender breeze, waving a greeting to them as they passed. A small flock of tiny Pine Siskin flew overhead chattering and chirping their well wishes for the journey.

Losa was the first to speak, abruptly barking the question that all yearned to ask, "What do you think your father will do when he learns that Chief Yanegwa has sent you, as his proxy, to the meeting?"

Onsi grunted agreement with the question. He was one of the few lighter-skinned members of the tribe. He took after his Prussian father, sporting blue eyes and dirty blonde hair. His face was narrow; his nose straight and pointed. Onsi's mother had fallen in love with a Prussian settler who had stumbled into the village twenty-four years ago, bleeding and injured from a bear attack. The tribe had taken him in, and Onsi's mother had nursed him back to health. Unfortunately, he had died suddenly when Onsi was a toddler. He had only flashes of memories of the blonde haired, blue-eyed man who stood half a foot taller than the average man in the tribe.

Shotek, who was walking to Losa's left with Onsi and Malili directly behind, turned his head to study Losa's serious face. He felt the weight of Chief Yanegwa's brightly-colored hair roach thud his back as it flopped back and forth in response to his movement.

"Are you asking because you fear for your life?" Shotek replied sarcastically.

"It crossed my mind," Losa answered.

Malili jumped into the conversation, "Do you not expect he will be angry?"

"I think he will join us," countered Onsi with a heavy sigh, "when he returns from the hunt."

"That is my greatest fear," exclaimed Losa. "I don't think I can take all the whining and complaining!"

Shotek shot Losa an icy glare. "Chief Yanegwa will tell him to stay home!" Shotek declared forcefully. He snapped his gaze forward and set his jaw. "The traveling party has been chosen. The chief's choice will stand!"

"So... you think you'll do better than your father?" questioned Losa, a doubtful tone saturiating his voice.

"Of course I will!" Shotek shot back. "My father does not think we should trade with the white settlers. The tribe agreed last night that we will. That is the position I will support. My father would never agree to that!"

An awkward hush fell on the group as they considered Shotek declaration.

"I admire you for that," said Malili breaking the silence after a few moments. "It is difficult to go against a parent... especially one as 'strong willed' as your father."

"He's not so bad..." Shotek replied hesitantly, "when you see all sides of him."

The group walked on. They were now only an hour from the southern pass that signaled the half-way point of their journey.

"What are these other sides of your father... those we have not seen?" Losa asked, again breaking the silence. He narrowed his eyes in response to a sudden intensification of Hashi's rays as a group of clouds scuttled out of her path.

Shotek squinted up at Hashi as he considered the best way to answer the question. "When we go into the forest to hunt... just the two of us... he is different. When he is away from the tribe... from the other men... he is quiet... more patient."

Shotek continued walking, but paused to collect his thoughts. He passed his spear from his left hand to his right, and stretched his long fingers to ease a cramp. "We've spent many summers... many mornings... many evenings hunting together. He taught me the best way to hold a blowgun," Shotek raised his hands in the air, gripping his spear as if it were a blowgun. "He showed me the best way to shape an arrow so it would fly straight and true. He taught me to hunt and track... to walk softly and silently in the forest."

Shotek continued with a longing in his voice and a far-away look in his eyes. "We spent many early mornings and late afternoons fishing. He taught me how to hold my spear," Shotek raised his right arm, spear and upper body positioned as if staring into the shallows of the Great River. "He showed me how to freeze my muscles and breath quietly... to wait patiently for the fish. To snap my wrist when I let loose the spear so it would cut quickly through the water."

"Hmph," Onsi grunted wistfully. Having never known his father, he would have liked to share those same experiences with him. Keeping with tradition, his mother's brother had taught him the ways of the tribe. His uncle was the only father Onsi had ever known.

Shotek stopped suddenly and turned to face the others. "My father really does care about the tribe," he admonished defensively.

"If that is true," Malili shot back, taking a step closer and striking a challenging pose, "he has an odd way of showing it!"

Losa pushed the two men apart and urged the group forward, "Let's keep moving. Hashi is already at the top of the sky."

"He does care!" Shotek continued. "He just thinks.... Look, he doesn't talk much about it, but his mother and sister, and several uncles - and many others in the tribe that he grew up in - died in the Great Sickness."

Shotek paused as if steeling himself to recount the details of an unpleasant story. "First they were consumed by heat, their whole bodies aching... bad headaches and shaking violently from chills. Then the vomiting started. My father says that after a few days his mother didn't even recognize him." He shook his head, and rubbed his long, strong fingers over his smooth, unwrinkled face. "Then she... they, got red bumps all over their eyes and faces... inside their mouths. The bumps grew bigger and filled up with yellow water. Many went blind. It spread all over their faces... their entire bodies." Shotek gulped, fighting down a rising nausea. "They lingered for days, writhing in pain." He closed his eyes and breathed deeply. "When death came... it was welcome."

"How horrible," breathed Onsi in disgust.

"Yes, that is horrible," agreed Losa. "But... what does that have to do with the white settlers?"

"A family of white men came to my father's village asking for help," Shotek answered. "One of their children had this illness. My grandmother helped them nurse the child. The child recovered, and the family left." Shotek attention was momentarily drawn to his left, distracted by a flock of birds that suddenly took flight from a tree, squawking and chittering at some unknown disturbance.

"Shortly after they left, my grandmother became ill." Shotek swung his gaze to meet Losa's, his face set in a somber, significant expression. "It was the same illness."

The group walked on in silence as each contemplated the meaning of the story.

It was Malili who broke the silence this time. "I understand how this must have affected your father. To see his mother and family, his tribe, suffer from this sickness. But... how is this the white man's fault? It is Hashi who brings illness and suffering - just as she brings joy and happiness. One man... one child cannot be held accountable for Hashi's choice."

"Yes, I agree," Shotek replied letting loose a long breath. "But, my father does not. And when he disagrees, he shouts. He does not know any other way. He thinks the loudest voice is the right one."

The group again fell silent considering Shotek's explanation, each step bringing them closer to the southern mountain pass.

"So, your father blames the white man for bringing disease," Losa summarized. "And that is why he is so against trading with them?"

"Yes. He thinks they will bring us a similar fate," Shotek answered. "He does not trust the white man, so he wants to keep them away."

"But you think we should trust them?" Malili questioned, jumping back into the conversation.

Shotek looked down, seemingly studying his feet as they strode over the grass-covered meadow floor. "I don't trust them," he said slowly, drawing out his words. "I don't trust them, but I don't think ignoring them will solve the problem."

The conversation was interrupted briefly by a flock of geese winging overhead honking loudly to encourage their formation leader. Shotek peered up and watched their progress as they moved across his field of vision.

"We can't ignore them," he continued, "any more than we can ignore those geese because we don't like how loud they are." He drew in a slow breath. "If we ignore the wolf, will he stopped hunting us? Can we stop the bear from digging up our crops by refusing to acknowledge that he exists?"

Shotek turned to meet the gazes of the men beside him. "The white settlers are now part of this valley... these mountains... this river." Gesturing broadly around at their surroundings he continued his oration, "They will not just go away if we pretend not to see them. Just as we must make peace with the wolf and the bear... with the rain and the lightening... we must make peace with them."

"Just like the chief says," Losa added, "...keep close the man you trust the least."

Onsi interrupted the conversation by pointing directly ahead. "The pass is just over this next rise. Let's stop at the Great Oak for our mid-day meal. I'm hungry."

The grouped nodded their agreement and picked up their pace.

Chapter 15

He was walking beside the Great River. The cool mountain water was tumbling and churning... unstopped by the rocks, the soil, the tree roots. The water grabbed him and swept him forward. He couldn't stop it. He was helpless. He started thrashing! He was sinking! Being pulled under...

Kisosen awoke with a start. He released a pent-up burst of air as he realized with relief that it was only a dream. He felt the warm rock beneath his cheek. The wind playfully tussled his hair. He felt Hashi's warm rays on the back of his now course gray and white hair.

"Oh no!" He bolted to a seated position, looking frantically around. Confusion flooded through him until he remembered that he was atop the standing rocks a little more than a mile south of the village.

He squinted up at Hashi. A third flood of terror washed over him as he realized that "It" had happened again. He had once again failed to awaken before Hashi, and now she was hanging low in the sky, mocking him and his clear disregard of his duties.

He covered his face with his hands and rubbed them vigorously over his lined and weathered skin. "Why do you torture me like this, Hashi!" he whispered in desperation. "I am an old man. I have been faithful to you," his plea tumbled from his lips. "I have stood fast for 12 winters, never once missing your awakenings or sleeps. Why is this happening now...?" his voice faded to nothing.

Kisosen labored to his feet, staggering a few steps before gaining his balance. He stood motionless on the rocks... his mind frozen... his heart heavy and thick with doubt. Finally he closed his heavy-lidded eyes and willed himself to breathe. In and out. In and out. He must regain control. It will do no good to panic.

"I must face the truth," Kisosen muttered to himself. "I am not the Kisosen. I am not the Hashi-bringer. I am a fake!"

He stumbled forward and then turned back and retraced his steps. "Or maybe..." he tried to tame his racing thoughts. "Maybe... it's all a lie."

He paced back and forth, looking down at the rocks and then up and Hashi. "It's a lie..." he mumbled. "The whole thing is a lie."

Stepping too close to the edge of the standing rocks, he slipped and fell again on his injured knee. He felt the wound crack open and blood well up and spill down his leg. "But it can't be?" he deliberated.

"My father would have told me. He was a good man."

Kisosen struggled to his feet and shook his fist at Hashi. "He would not keep this from me! Something so important! He would have told me!" he shouted.

Kisosen suddenly felt weak all over and sank slowly to a seated position on the rocks. He wrapped his arms protectively around his knees, his head resting on a forearm. His mind went blank. His heart thudded so loudly it drowned out the sounds of the birds, the crickets, and the wind. He concentrated on just breathing in and out.

Sometime later, Kisosen lifted his head in response to a distant calling. 'Was that the wind keening over the rocks? ' He tilted an ear toward the sound. Gradually the keening turned into the sound of Chaska's clear, unwavering voice calling his name.

"Father! Are you there?"

A moment later Chaska young, strong face appeared over the edge of the rocks as he climbed the rough path to the top.

"Father!" Chaska rushed to his side wrapping a supportive arm around his shoulders. "Father, I've been looking for you for hours!"

Chaska then noticed the torn knee of Kisosen's trousers soaked through with fresh and dried blood. "You are injured! What happened? Can you walk?"

Kisosen waved Chaska away, "It is nothing more than a scratch. I fell coming down the mountain this morning. The wolves..."

Kisosen wrestled with his thoughts. 'Do I tell him the truth? Did my father have the same struggle? Are we just replaying the same scene over and over? My grandfather knew and chose not to tell his son. My father knew, and chose not to tell me. Now I know... do I tell my son?'

"Father," Chaska stirred him from his anxieties. "You are clearly not well. Let's get you back to the hut. Hialeah will know what to do."

Chapter 16

Mali humma waited... again. Always waiting for his prey. Always waiting for his destiny. 'But,' he thought with anticipation, 'after today there will be no more waiting. His time was here! This was the day he stopped waiting... and started living!'

The cry of Tanampi's hawk jerked him from his revelry. An onrush of adrenaline flooded his veins. He checked the arrow again, ensuring that it was perfectly nocked on the string of his bow. His brother's words had centered him. His mind was calm and focused.

When the party finally crested the rise, his heart gave a startled thump, so loud he was sure they must have heard, even though they were still 100 yards away.

A gush of rage filled him momentarily when he spotted Yanegwa's distinctive ceremonial hair roach and the colorful turkey feathers of his cape. He pushed down his anger, regaining his focus.

He silently sucked in a long, deep breath. Holding the breath, he rapidly drew back the bow, his upper back and shoulder muscles flexing with the effort. The Catawba arrow rested innocently on the side of his callused finger. He set his shoulders. Finding the rhythm of the group's pace, Mali humma aimed at where Yanegwa would be after the second it took the arrow to fly.

He released the arrow with a satisfied hiss of breath.

A second later, he heard the startled cry of pain. The arrow found it's mark in the dead center of Yanegwa's chest. The chief was flung back into Losa. A shriek of angry howls crescendoed from the group.

Mali humma, realizing there was no time to gloat, threw himself from the tree. He hit the ground at a full run. The adrenaline from the successful shot gave him a surge of power as he sprinted through the trees and toward the eastern ridge where he would meet with his brother by mid-afternoon. There would be time for celebration then!

Chapter 17

Kisosen was woken by the sounds of angry shouts and a women's shriek of disbelief and lament. Slowly blinking his eyes to focus them, he looked around his family's village hut in search of the sound. Pushing himself onto one elbow, he realized the commotion was coming from outside.

When Kisosen pushed through the buckskin door of the hut, the scene that greeted him was chaotic. A crowd had gathered in the central plaza. Men were shouting, waving their arms, and gesturing angrily. Some women had hands covering their faces. Others were comforting a small group who were on their knees singing the traditional death lament, repeating a name over and over. Children were huddled together wearing shocked and frightened expressions.

Kisosen pushed forward, straining to hear the name being sung in the death lament. 'Who died?' he wondered. 'And what kind of death would cause such a commotion?'

He shuffled forward toward the group of men clustered around what must be the fallen tribal member. Disbelief washed over him when he recognized, through the legs of the crowd, Chief Yanegwa's distinctive and colorful turkey feather cape and hair roach.

"No!" he cried. "It cannot be!" He had warned the chief. Surely he would not allow himself to be killed! What purpose would that serve!

He thrust himself through the crowd until he was standing over his friend's lifeless body. An intense moment of disorientation washed over him as he slowly realized that the face was too young, the hair too black and shiny, the torso under the cape, too muscular. He blinked his eyes rapidly and willed them to study the dead man's face.

"Shotek!" he hissed.

He searched the young, innocent face and his mind went blank. His heart seemed to stop -- each drop of blood in his body seemed to freeze. He staggered back. Strong arms reached out to keep him upright. Pushing them away he spun on the spot searching for the lined and weathered face of his old friend.

Directly behind him he locked eyes with Chief Yanegwa. The two men stiffened as they stared at each other. Anger dripped from Yanegwa's eyes as they sought understanding. He motioned to Kisosen to follow him to the Council House.

Kisosen stumbled after the chief as he angrily flung the buckskin door aside and stormed into the Council House. When Kisosen finally passed into the round stone walls of the house he found Yanegwa pacing irritably around the now smoldering and banked central fire.

"How could this happen!" Yanegwa hissed fiercely.

Kisosen paused in confusion, shaking his head from side to side. "What did happen?"

"Shotek!" the chief spat. "Shotek was murdered!"

"But... how..." Kisosen stammered. "I do not understand..."

"You said if I went to the Council Meeting I would die." Chief Yanegwa said accusingly. "You did not say I would be murdered! That anyone who went in my place would be murdered!"

Kisosen sucked in a long breath and tried to make sense of the situation. It suddenly dawned on him why his confusion was so great. "Why is Shotek wearing your cape and hair roach?"

The chief stopped his pacing and clutched his head in both hands. Tilting his head back, he closed his eyes and breathed deeply, as if trying to regain control.

"You said I should not go to the meeting," the chief muttered. "How was I to know!" He threw his hands up in disbelief and then resumed his pacing. "Did you know this would happen?" the chief pleaded. "Did you know? Did Hashi say?"

Kisosen repeated his question, "Why was Shotek wearing your cape and hair roach?"

Chief Yanegwa stopped and stared at Kisosen as if just realizing he was asking a question.

"Why was Shotek wearing your cape and hair roach!?" Kisosen said louder, his anger now growing.

"I sent him as my proxy," the chief answered. "You said I must not go... but the tribe needed representation. Someone had to go in my place!"

"But... why Shotek?"

The chief shook his head slowly from side to side and scrubbed his hands again over his hair. He had pulled several gray hairs from his topknot, and they sprouted erratically from his head accentuating his look of turmoil and agitation.

"Shotek has a good heart... had a good heart," the chief corrected himself. "He may have cowered in his father's shadow, but he did not share in his darkness."

The chief's pacing slowed and his steps became labored. "I wanted to build his confidence. I wanted to send his father a message. I wanted Shotek to find his own voice. To wanted the entire tribe to see that Shotek was different!"

The chief sank wearily down by the banked fire and put his head in his hands. Kisosen lowered himself stiffly down beside him.

"But, why was he wearing your cape and hair roach?" Kisosen again asked more gently, clearly moved by his friend's emotional turmoil.

The chief raised his gaze to meet Kisosen's. "He wanted a symbol of his authority to speak for me... to represent the tribe," he explained. "What better symbol than my cape and hair roach?"

A wave of nausea swept over Kisosen as the final pieces of the situation fell into place. His vision went temporarily black. He swayed noticeably where he sat.

"Itanale!" the chief hissed as he grabbed Kisosen's arm to steady him. "What is it?"

A myriad of jumbled thoughts swarmed through Kisosen's mind like a horde of angry wasps. "No..." he whispered. "No, this cannot be."

"What cannot be!" demanded the chief. "What are you not telling me!"

Kisosen was silent for several minutes as he tried to quiet his racing mind and heart. He felt Chief Yanegwa's accusing stare bore through his skull. 'Was this the time for truth,' he thought, "Or was this another secret he would take to the next life?'

"I was not honest with you," he said closing his eyes and letting out a long, resigned breath. "I was sleeping in the meadow. I heard two men plotting to kill you during your journey to the regional meeting.

They said they would hide in the Great Oak by the southern pass and shoot you with a Catawba arrow."

Kisosen's voice dropped to a whisper. "I never thought... never ever thought that you would send someone in your place... someone dressed in your cape and wearing your hair roach."

Kisosen dropped his head in both hands in shame and despair. "I never dreamed you would send Shotek...."

"Two men?" the chief repeated. "Could you tell who they were? Did you recognize their voices?"

Kisosen paused, collecting his strength. "It was Mali humma and Tanampi."

Chapter 18

It was early evening when the two brothers saw the rugged edge of the northern palisade. Although exhausted, Mali humma still felt light on his feet. The trials and hardships of the journey only made the victory sweeter. He paused tilting an ear toward the village. Faint cries of lament and mourning drifted toward them on the evening breeze.

A deep feeling of satisfaction emanated through Mali humma's chest. He checked himself, and wrestled a look of concern onto his face. The speech he had practiced began to play again in his head.

'Chief Yanegwa? Dead? How is this possible? Who could have done this? The Catawba? Never! Even they could not be so evil! Well, if the chief had not angered him so, he and Tanampi would have been in the traveling party. The Catawba would not have attacked such a well-armed party! The chief would still be alive!' Mali humma again tested the muscles of his face, working purposefully to find that perfect look of deep shock and concern.

As the two brothers entered the hamlet through the north gate, the bear skin strapped on Tanampi's back, it was clear that something terrible had happened. Instead of the expected greetings of return, the villagers gathered in the central plaza wore expressions of sympathy and concern, quickly averting their eyes.

Mali humma's gaze swung instantly to the Council House looking for the bowed and huddled bodies of the tribe's women who should be singing Yanegwa's song of lament. The men of the village should all have ashes in their hair... but he did not see any.

Sweeping his eyes around the village, Mali humma all of a sudden realized with a shock that the mourning wails were not coming from the Council House, but instead from his own. He rushed forward, no longer having to fake the look of concern.

His mother-in-law, wife, and daughter lay prostrate on the ground in front of the hut, consumed in the deepest well of grief. Mali humma's wife looked up as he approached, her bloodshot eyes blank and unseeing.

"What has happened!" he hissed, grabbing his wife's shoulders and giving them a shake. "What has happened!"

"Shotek," his wife moaned, her head snapping back and forth as he shook her.

"Shotek..." Mali humma replied in confusion. "What do you mean, Shotek?"

Winona reached up from her place of mourning and wrapped her arms around Mali humma's leg, "They killed him, Father!" she wailed. "They killed Shotek!"

Mali humma's muscles froze, then a wave of nausea and dizziness made him stagger. "Shotek," he croaked. "Shotek…"

He stumbled forward, throwing back the buckskin covering the door, and ducked awkwardly into the hut. It took a moment for his eyes to adjust. The horror of his only son's lifeless body slowly emerged in front of his eyes. First the edges came into focus. Then his clothing. Then his face. His eyes were closed. His mouth gaped open as if in a cry of shock and pain. The Catawba arrow shaft still embedded, had been broken off three inches from his chest, which was ominously covered in dried blood. The turkey feather cape had been removed, but Chief Yanegwa's hair roach still perched mockingly on his head.

Mali humma suddenly found himself on the ground beside his son's body. He could not breathe. He could not see. A piercing keen lacerated his ears. It was a moment before he realized the sound was coming from his own lips.

Chapter 19

    Keeping with tradition, Mali humma's family was required to mourn for seven days under the direction of the village shaman. To fully cleanse their spirits, they were to stay away from the other villagers, restrict their intake of food and water, and refrain from expressing strong emotions such as anger or joy. The women of the family sang the death lament, repeating Shotek's name over and over. The men covered their hair with ashes.

    That evening, Shotek's body was washed with water and boiled willow root then anointed with lavender oil, which was believed to cleanse the body of impurities. An eagle feather was placed on the body which was then wrapped in the bearskin that Mali humma and Tanampi had brought home that evening.

    While Shotek's family prepared their son for burial, Chief Yanegwa called the members of the tribe together in the Council House. One by one, Onsi, Losa, and Malili related the details of Shotek's death. They described the Catawba arrow dropping blindly from the sky, Shotek's last labored breaths, and the futile chase of unseen ghosts through the forest.

The adults of the tribe, huddled in the Council House, debating their response to Shotek's murder well past Hashi-sleep. Chief Yanegwa sat in silence, listening.

"We cannot do nothing!" Losa proclaimed forcefully. "They intended to kill our chief. This is war!"

"We must strike!" Malili agreed, leading an assenting chorus of voices.

Chief Yanegwa held up his hands to silence the group. "Malili, you chased the warrior who initiated the strike. Did you see any part of him? Can you verify that he was Catawba?"

Malili looked down studying his hands. He opened and closed his fists several times. "No."

"But, it was a Catawba arrow!" Losa reproached. "That's proof enough!"

Another assenting chorus rose from the group, many others striking an agreeing chord with Losa.

This time it was Chaska who raised his hands to still the riotous group. "Do you not remember the butchery of the last war with the Catawba? We turned the earth red with the blood of our, and their men. What did it accomplish?"

Chaska swung his dark, piercing eyes around the group, meeting the gaze of key members of the tribal council. "We cannot start another war because of one arrow."

"Even if that arrow was intended for me," the chief added.

The group fell silent considering Chaska's words and struggling with their anger.

Chief Yanegwa offered a compromise, "We will take this matter with us to the Regional Council Meeting."

"But, we've missed the meeting. It starts tomorrow!" Malili interjected.

"Onsi, Losa, Malili, Chaska," the chief made eye contact with each man as he said his name. "Tomorrow we will leave for the meeting. If we make haste, we will be there for the evening ceremony. The first day of these meeting are largely ceremonial. There will still be two days to discuss the business at hand."

The men and women of the council exchanged skeptical and resigned glances.

"It is late," the chief said with a heavy sigh. "We leave at Hashi-wake. Let's all get some sleep."

On the mountain earlier that evening, instead of taking his stance to put Hashi to bed, Kisosen sat dejectedly on the western edge of the plaza and just watched Hashi sink into the earth without his guidance.

'Proof,' he said to himself. 'Proof of the lie.'

Hashi never needed him. His role was nothing but pomp and pageantry. Six miles a day of useless promenade, up and down the mountain. One hundred and eighty miles of wasted energy every full moon. That time would have been better spent hunting, fishing, protecting the crops... feeling the warmth of his wife's body pressed up against his, instead of the long, cold nights alone on the mountain.

"This must end," he muttered to himself. The tribe needs to know the truth. He could not, in good conscious, pass the burden of this lie onto Chaska.

Early the next day, just as Hashi's golden rays were creeping over the tops of the oak, hickory, and red maple on the valley floor, the shaman began Shotek's funeral with a traditional prayer.

> *I give you this one thought to keep.*
> *I'm with you still; I do not sleep.*
> *I am a thousand winds that blow.*
> *I am the diamond glints on snow.*
> *I am the sunlight on ripened grain.*
> *I am the gentle autumn rain.*
> *When you awaken in the morning hush,*
> *I am the swift, uplifting rush,*
> *Of quiet birds in circled flight,*
> *I am the soft stars that shine at night.*
> *Do not think of me as gone.*
> *I am with you still, in each new dawn.*
> *Do not stand at my grave and weep.*
> *I am not there, I do not sleep.*
> *Do not stand there at my grave and cry.*
> *I am not there, I did not die.*

After the shaman offered his final prayers and spiritual lessons to the family, Shotek's uncles heaved the body onto their shoulders and carried it to the far eastern edge of the tribal fields tucked in the shadow of the mountains. In a somber silence, they buried the body in a shallow grave and covered it with a thick layer of stones.

All of Shotek's possessions were buried with him. The 59 inch long Black Locust bow his father had helped him shape with bear oil and season with fire... the carefully stitched elk-skin quiver that held his arrows, meticulously crafted from cane sticks, flint, and feathers... his rivercane blowgun and locust blow darts feathered with thistle down. After the burial the shaman returned to the family hut and cleansed it of bad spirits with teas and lavender oil.

Chapter 20

The next four days was difficult for all. Mali humma's family remained in seclusion in their hut. The men of the tribe patrolled the fields, forests, and meadows within five miles of the village in anticipation of another Catawba attack. The entire village was on edge anxiously waiting for Chief Yanegwa and the traveling party's safe return.

Kisosen isolated himself on the mountain, coming down only for the mid-day meal. He was not worried about Chaska or Chief Yanegwa's safety. He knew that the murderer had already been caught and was suffering a punishment worse than death.

His only concern was what the chief would do about it when he returned. After he had confessed that it was Mali humma and Tanampi that had plotted the murder, the anger that spewed from the chief was greater than any emotion he had ever witnessed.

When Mali humma returned from his 'hunt' that evening, it took all of the chief's strength and control to not execute Mali humma on the spot. They had agreed that executing Mali humma would be too merciful for this crime. Having to live with the fact that he had killed his only son would be a much greater punishment than anything else the tribe could ever do.

Kisosen's mind was a dark tangle of emotion. Concern over what the chief would do when he returned. A profound flood of guilt over his failure to tell the chief the whole story. A weighty emptiness at the acknowledgement of his useless role as the Kisosen. And an intense anger at the chief. Why did he have to give Shotek his cape and hair roach? If Shotek had not been wearing these, Mali humma would never have shot the arrow! Shotek would still be walking his path in this life.

To make matter worse, how was he to resolve the issue with Hashi? Should he just tell Chaska? Should he reveal the truth to the whole tribe? If he did, though, what would be their reaction?

They would think he'd gone mad. That he had surrendered to the burden of his role. That twelve winters of managing Hashi had softened his mind and spirit. They would 'retire' him. Then, Chaska would assume this burden, and the whole cycle would just repeat itself.

It was a most difficult problem... and four days of wrestling with it alone on the mountain did not make the solution any clearer.

Chapter 21

On the mornings of the sixth and seventh day after Shotek's murder, the shaman led Mali humma and his family to the grave site. The women wailed. Mali humma bowed his head and dropped to his knees beside the stones covering his only son. Silently, he begged Shotek for forgiveness. He promised him he was a changed man.

The afternoon of the seventh day brought an end to the family's official mourning period. Keeping with tradition, they joined the entire tribe in the central plaza that evening for the death ceremony, designed to help Shotek complete his long journey to the Spirit World.

Led by Chief Yanegwa -- who had returned with the traveling party from the regional council meeting the previous evening -- the members of the tribe offered their condolences to Shotek's family. All feasted on roasted deer and a variety of side dishes, each one brought by a different tribal family. A plate for Shotek was offered, heaped high with food, herbs, and gifts to ensure a safe journey into the after-life.

After the meal, a select group of villagers, wearing turtle-shell leg rattles, performed the ceremonial death dance around a sacred fire. The remaining villagers kept time with drums and gourd rattles. Kisosen watched the proceedings from a distance, spurning his seat on the bench next to the chief and the shaman.

After the dance, Chief Yanegwa rose from the bench, positioned himself in front of the fire, and extended his hands to quiet the group.

"Brothers and sisters!" he said raising his voice to be heard above the din of the group. "This has been a most challenging time. But, I am pleased to report that the regional council was a success. The tribes in attendance agreed to trade with the white settlers and have set terms for these interactions."

A cheer rose up from the villagers to show their pleasure. This would mean more access to the white man's goods including: horses, hoes, axes, woven fabric, steel pots, guns, knives, whiskey, and rum.

"In addition," Chief Yanegwa continued, "I have a story to share. While it is not a traditional part of this type of celebration, I believe it will be of great value."

Puzzled glances were exchanged while the villagers settled themselves around the sacred fire in the central hearth. The older men and women took seats on the benches while the younger found places on the ground. The children clustered around their mothers and aunts. The chief paced in a circle around the fire waiting for the group to settle and then began his story.

"There once was a Big Buck with an enormous rack," Chief Yanegwa raised his arms over his head, with his fingers spread and his palms spaced about three feet apart.

"Big Buck was mighty and had a mystical ability to avoid injury or death. He was feared and respected by many creatures of the forest... but he was not happy."

The chief began to slowly circle the fire, motioning to illustrate each point of his story, catching the eyes of each villager one by one in turn. The rhythm of his feet on the plaza stones kept time with the chant of his voice as he unfurled his tale.

"Big Buck was not happy because he was filled with jealousy and envy! He was not satisfied being the biggest, strongest, and mightiest buck in the forest. He not only wanted to be the chief of all bucks - he wanted to be the chief of the entire forest!" A murmur traveled through the villagers as they exchanged whispered feelings about the buck. The fire popped loudly and sent up a well-time plume of smoke as a particularly green section of wood began to burn.

"The real chief of the forest was the strong and powerful Great Cougar. He was as long as a canoe and as tall as a man's hip." A twitter of excitement percolated through the tribe as they all envisioned a 225 pound, nine-foot long mountain cougar with two inch incisors who could leap as high as 16 feet and over a 45 foot wide span.

"Big Buck spent much of his time stomping through the forest, shaking his mighty antlers at everyone he saw, and plotting how he might defeat Great Cougar." With this, the children giggled with delight as the chief puffed out his chest, stamped his feet, and shook his head donning an exaggerated look of smug self-importance.

"Great Cougar knew of Big Buck's desire to be chief. He knew the buck was strong and mighty and could run as fast as the wind. He knew of him, and he respected him." Here Chief Yanegwa paused and looked up to the western sky, squinting at Hashi as she slowly sunk toward her bed.

"But, even though Great Cougar respected Big Buck, he knew the buck could never be chief. It takes more than strength and speed to be chief. It takes more than skill at the hunt. Being chief is not about being the loudest, the most voluble, or the most pompous. Being chief is not about arrogance, or conceit, or swagger."

The villagers were truly mesmerized now. A few of them sat back and cocked their heads in puzzlement. They looked at the back of Mali humma's bent and grieving head. While they saw the clear connection between him and Big Buck, they all wondered -- what does this have to do with Shotek's death?

"Many creatures of the forest complained about Big Buck," continued the chief, " asking Great Cougar to punish him or send him away. They could not see why he tolerated the buck's arrogance."

"But Great Cougar, in his wisdom, had faith in Hashi. He had faith in the moon, and the winds, and the rains. He had faith in the stars. He had faith that the great Universe finds a way to bring balance to everything. When one thing is excessive, the Universe creates something to pull it down. If another thing is too small, the Universe finds a way to build it up. Great Cougar knew that it was not his place to find a way to balance Big Buck's hatred, greed, and jealousy. He could not wash deep and clean the buck's soul. Only the most powerful act by the most powerful spirit could do that."

Chief Yanegwa paced slowly around the circle letting the tension build. Then he drew in a long, slow breath and continued with his story. "Now, something I have not told you is that Big Buck had a son. He was as large as his father, but he cowered in his father's shadow. The burden of his father's hate and envy made his hooves heavy and clumsy. His body was strong, but his will was weak. He wanted desperately to make his father proud, but he did not know how."

The tribe was deadly quiet now. Only the crackle and occasional pop of the fire could be heard. Even the crickets and birds had stopped singing. Hashi had stopped moving in the sky. All leaned in, hanging on the chief's words.

"One evening as Hashi was just slipping into bed and the darkness was creeping quickly over the mountain casting great black shadows under the trees, Great Cougar settled himself down in the long grasses of a meadow, looking to catch his dinner. He was hungry."

"Big Buck, picking his way quietly through the forest, saw the cougar enter his hiding place. He was instantly filled with rage!" Yanegwa reached over and dropped a pile of kindling and dry grasses on the fire causing it to burst into a swell of crackling flames and send a whoosh of smoke billowing into the sky. A ripple of excitement ran through the crowd.

"Big Buck knew he could not defeat Great Cougar by himself. Why did he have to be born a deer! Why could he not have claws and sharp teeth! Why had Hashi insulted him so with these dull, grinding molars! Big Buck turned and stamped away from the meadow. There must be some way to defeat this cougar. Then he, Big Buck, would be chief!"

"Big Buck marched through the forest, willing himself to form a plan." The chief paused, head down, hands behind his back, pacing agitatedly around the fire. He let a full minute go by, as he imitated Big Buck lost deep in thought.

Suddenly and violently, the chief turned and snapped his head up high. "Then, it hit him! Hashi sent him an inspiration - like one of her great lightning bolts!" Yanegwa's voice was filled with excitement.

"Big Buck turned in a circle, scenting the air. Where were those irksome wolves? They were always harassing him. He was always spurring them to take action, trying to get them to end the chief's reign. He knew that they were the only beings of the forest capable of taking down a cougar. If he could goad them now into chasing him, he could run straight through the meadow leaping with skill and grace over Great Cougar! The wolves would run right into the chief and there would be a mighty fight. We would see who would prevail - the chief alone, or the pack of wolves!"

"Big Buck, now very pleased with himself, strode off confidently following the scent of the wolves." Yanegwa again paused, this time reaching for the cup of sassafras tea held for him by his wife. He took a long drink and gave Ghigau a nod of thanks. She returned the nod and took back the cup. The chief then continued the story.

"It took some time, but Big Buck finally found the wolves. They were stalking through a different meadow nearly half a mile away from Great Cougar. The buck knew that he had to find a way to fool the pack into chasing him. Many times before, he had easily out-paced their chase and they had grown discouraged. If they were to chase him for half a mile, he would need to make them believe they had a chance of catching him. As he grew closer to the pack, he started limping and hanging his head like he was in pain."

The chief now started hobbling and put a painful grimace on his face. He let out a moan of pain and stumbled a bit for effect.

"After a few moments, Big Buck sensed the pack had seen him. He threw up his head in feigned surprise and met the yellow, scowling eyes of the wicked alpha male of the pack."

Now the chief struck a pose to mimic the alpha wolf. He bent over and glared menacingly at a row of young children. They all yelped and cowered together in entertained fear. The sound of satisfied chuckles radiated from the adults in the tribe.

"Big Buck paused for a second, then leaped away from the pack running at half speed toward the meadow where Great Cougar laid waiting."

"The chase was most thrilling! Big Buck would speed ahead just a bit, and then stumble and slow until the pack was within a few feet of his tail. He would then heave himself forward creating a little space, then pretend to falter again. The pack surged forward in hungry anticipation. They had never gotten so close to Big Buck! Their mouths were already salivating in anticipation of savory deer meat!"

The villagers were all leaning forward eagerly. Many had risen to their knees. It was one of the most thrilling stories Chief Yanegwa had ever told.

"Now, something I have not told you," said the chief, causing an instant groan to ripple through the crowd, "is that unbeknownst to Big Buck, his son, Young Buck, was still awake -- even at this time of night -- and was picking his way slowly through the forest, still grazing on tender shoots and grasses." A collective gasp emitted from the tribe. They all knew that normally at this time, deer hunkered down in tall grasses, brush, or dense foliage where they were not visible or exposed. A young deer alone on the mountain could easily fall prey to many night-time hunters.

"Tragically," continued the chief, "Young Buck's path was leading him directly across the path that his father was now leading the wolf pack along." Chief Yanegwa brought the tips of his fingers directly toward each other ending with the two palm edges crossed, then paused dramatically to let the implication sink in.

"The story now turns so sad, that I cannot share the details. But when the wolves saw Young Buck, they -- angry with Big Buck for continually harassing them and trying to use them to do his dirty work -- turned instead toward Young Buck. They chased him down, and killed him."

Chief Yanegwa gazed up to the sky with a deep and sorrowful look on his face. He continued in a heavy and monotone voice. "Thrilled by the chase, his senses deadened by his hatred, and overcome with jealousy and envy, Big Buck ran on, not even seeing his son or knowing that he was in danger. He executed his graceful and mighty leap over Great Cougar and ran on through the forest until he reached the safety of a thick field of tall grass and settled smugly and haughtily down to sleep."

A great sigh escaped the tribe as they collectively let out the breath they were holding. A moment of silence past as the purpose of the story struck them.

For the first time Mali humma raised his head. He locked eyes with Chief Yanegwa. The chief lowered his chin. A message flew between them.

'I know what you did,' Yanegwa's silent message flashed into Mali humma's mind. 'Your hatred and jealousy did not kill me; it killed your son.'

Chapter 22

   The tribe broke up slowly after the chief's story, drifting in pairs and trios back to their huts. Kisosen found himself alone on a back bench. Chief Yanegwa and Ghigau had retired to the Council House. Chaska and Hialeah had drifted toward their hut. Suddenly, his granddaughter was at his knee, a tentative hand resting gently on his thigh.

   He dropped stiffly to one knee and gathered the child closely into his arms, feeling the softness of her hair pressed tightly to his cheek. "I love you Ahyoka," he whispered into her ear. "You are my favorite granddaughter."

   She patted his back and giggled. "I am your only granddaughter!"

   "Yes, but you will always be my first granddaughter, and that is something special."

That evening was gentle with a cool, light breeze, but Kisosen's mind was still in turmoil. As he ambled toward the mountain, he turned the chief's story over in his mind. He was silently in awe of how the chief had crafted the perfect message. Clear enough for Mali humma and Tanampi to read without fail, but subtle enough for the rest of the tribe to be left wondering what it was really about.

Kisosen contemplated the most important part of the story. Yes, it was true. It wasn't his or the chief's role to find a way to balance Mali humma's hatred, greed, or jealousy. Only Hashi could do that. He let out a long sigh. One so deep it seemed to come from some far-away place. With that sigh, the guilt and anger he had been carrying flowed from him like a river washing clean a storm-ravaged shore.

It was at that moment he realized that Hashi had, in fact, found the perfect way to level Mali humma's greed and jealousy -- and to wash clean his soul. If he had told the chief precisely what was to happen... if they had exposed Mali humma's treachery to the tribe... if they had banned him from the village... had censured him... no balance would have been achieved. He would still be filled with loathing and bitterness. And he would not have stopped. His hatred and envy was so deep, he would have hunted Yanegwa down just to have his revenge. Forcing Mali humma to kill his own son was the only way to transform him. It was a cruel, but powerful gift.

When Kisosen finally stepped onto the plaza at the top of Tanawha Mountain, Hashi was just dipping her toe into her bed. Out of habit, he strode to the west side of the plaza, planted his feet, and raise his arms. He watched in silence as she continued inching into her bed.

With his anger and guilt washed away, he was finally able to see more clearly the solution to his other problem. At that moment, he made the decision that he would not tell the tribe about his discovery. They were not ready. And it was not fair to them. Their beliefs were so strong, and gave them so much comfort. It gave them peace to think they had some control over their environment. It was an integral part of their spiritual wellness.

But he would tell Chaska. He must spare him the confusion and disillusionment. He must tell him the truth. He would bring him to the mountain top sometime soon and they would sit here together and watch Hashi sink into her bed all on her own. He would make sure that Chaska understood. Together they would figure out what to do.

Slowly, a distant recollection seeped into his mind from the corners of his memory. He remembered a strange conversation he'd had with his own father, thirteen winters ago sitting atop Tanawha Mountain, almost in exactly the spot in which he stood.

"Itanale," his father had said. "Your role as the Kisosen is more complex than you realize. Always remember...

> *To honor is to serve.*
> *To serve is to honor.*
> *To control is a fallacy,*
> *The dishonorable call a service."*

Kisosen stood rooted to the stone of the mountain reflecting on those words. At that moment he realized his father **had** tried to tell him the truth. Itanale was just not wise enough to hear it.

"Thank you, Hashi," he whispered. "Thank you for helping me to see the truth."

A soft, sage-like voice reverberated distantly in his head. *'Itanale... you are the Kisosen, the Hashi bringer. But you must realize, there are many ways to 'bring.'*

A long moment passed as the wind keened across the plaza, swirling dried leaves around Kisosen's feet.

'You must let go,' the voice breathed in his head. *'Trust me. Have faith in the Universe. Have faith in how things are meant to be....'*

Kisosen squeezed his eyes shut willing Hashi to keep speaking. *'To control is a fallacy the dishonorable call a service. But trust and faith allow one to truly serve,'* the voice echoed softly.

Kisosen's eyes snapped opened to see the last curve of Hashi's head just suspended over the tip of the furthest western mountain. *'I do not need a keeper. I need a friend....'*

Hashi's form was gone, but the last glows of her light sent a burst of radiant color across the sky. *'While I do not need you to help me rise or sleep, I appreciate that you are there. It gives me comfort to look upon your face before I slip into my bed each night. Knowing that you will be there in the morning gives me peace as I move through the darkness. I can only hope that you feel the same about me.'*

Kisosen watched the last rays of Hashi's light fade gently from the sky as she slipped fully into her bed.

"Ah," he whispered in reply. "I think I've finally learned the secret."

Story Notes

Where is the Story Set?

If you like a good puzzle, the story provides several clues. Consider these facts, and turn the page when you think you know the answer.

- ○ The tribal village is in a valley three miles from the top of Tanawha Mountain, and Kisosen descends and climbs this mountain each day. That must mean that the elevation change between the top of the mountain and the valley is not too significant.

- ○ The tribe grows corn (among other crops) in the valley. Corn grows best in a climate that offers warm weather and long, sun-filled days. That must mean that the valley is at a low enough elevation, and in a place that experiences a long, relatively warm summer. These two facts, together, indicate that Tanawha Mountain is a fairly low mountain, possibly between 3000 and 5000 feet (or 1000 to 1500 meters) and positioned in a part of the world that experiences a fairly temperate climate.

- o   Red Spruce and Fraser Fir grow on the mountain, while oak, hickory, and red maple are prevalent in the valley.

- o   Flowers in the area include: lily of the valley, spoonleaf sundew, bellwort and goldenrod, pink flowering Rosebay rhododendrons, flowering trillium, lady slippers, japonicas, jack-in-the-pulpits, wild ginger, evening primrose, and mountain laurel.

- o   The tribe collects roots, berries, crab apples, nuts, acorns, wild potatoes, and zamia roots.

- o   Animals in the area include: white-tailed deer, fish, wild turkeys, raccoons, black bears, wolves, cougars, elk, river trout, rabbit, possum, and porcupine.

- o   Birds include: Wood Thrush, Tufted Titmouse, Pine Siskin, and geese.

Another small clue offered is the era of the story setting: the mid 1700's. White settlers are in the area, growing in numbers, and trade is becoming more common. The tribe is concerned enough to warrant a gathering of local tribes to discuss the issue.

Turn the page when you think you know where the story might be set.

Answer to Story Setting

Given the clues stated above, the most likely setting is in the United States in either eastern Tennessee or western North Carolina.

The city of Asheville, North Carolina is set in a large, meandering valley surrounded by the Blue Ridge Mountains - a fairly low range of mountains.

Mount Mitchell is the highest peak in that range (and in fact the highest peak east of the Mississippi) at 6,684 feet (2,037 m). In that area, about 125 peaks exceed 5,000 feet (1,500 m) and there are 39 peaks in North Carolina and Tennessee higher than 6,000 feet (1,800 m).[1] Many rivers run through this area as well. This valley is a very possible setting.

Asheville has a temperate climate. Summer highs are around 85 degrees Fahrenheit (29 C). Winters are fairly mild with average January lows at 28 degrees Fahrenheit (-2 C). The growing season is approximately early April to late October.

---

[1] See Wikipedia: Blue Ridge Mountains.
https://en.wikipedia.org/wiki/Blue_Ridge_Mountains

The history of the Asheville, North Carolina area also fits the ancillary facts of the story. A permanent settlement of European immigrants was created in 1785. The surrounding area was dubbed Buncombe county in late 1791. The settlement was officially named Asheville, after then Governor Samuel Ashe, in 1797.[2]

Which Tribe is the Village?

Based on the proposed setting of Asheville, North Carolina and the era of the mid-1700's, the tribe that most closely matches the majority of the story elements is Cherokee. I have tried to stay true to the historical and cultural facts of that tribe whenever possible, but have borrowed from other tribes as needed.

Cherokee History in Asheville, NC

Before European settlers came to the Asheville, North Carolina area, that land was within the boundaries of the Cherokee Nation. "At its height, the Cherokee Nation ranged from the Appalachian Mountains to the Mississippi River, and from the Ohio River to the Piedmont of present-day Georgia and Alabama, an estimated area of 100,000 square miles."[3]

---

[2] See: http://www.ashevillenc.com/area_info/history_of_asheville

[3] The Cherokee Before 1800. About North Georgia. Found on June 17, 2016 at: http://www.aboutnorthgeorgia.com/ang/The_Cherokee

In 1540 the Spanish explorer Hernando de Soto brought the first European visitors to what is now the Asheville, NC area. Along with these Europeans came smallpox and other diseases which seriously depleted the tribe's population.[4]

From the early 1600's through the early 1700's, the Cherokee had relatively peaceful and regular contact with the European immigrants in the area, including trading goods. Smallpox epidemics and military campaigns continued to devastate the Cherokee population and destroyed dozens of Cherokee towns. "Seventy-five percent of Cherokee land was lost through treaties." The European settlers and the Cherokee nation had an uneasy relationship for most of the 1700's.[5]

Tragically, around 1838, the majority of the Cherokee were driven from this area (including Georgia, North Carolina, and Tennessee) and forced to travel to Oklahoma along a route that has become known as the "Trail of Tears." Twenty five to fifty percent of the remaining Cherokee population died during this period.[6]

---

[4] "Cherokee History, Part One" (text/.html). Lee Sultzman. 28 February 1996. Archived from the original on July 7, 2006. Retrieved 2006-07-23.

[5] Cherokee History in the North Carolina Mountains. Found on June 17, 2016 at: http://www.blueridgeheritage.com/heritage/cherokee/cherokee-history

[6] Trail of Tears. Found on June 17, 2016 at: http://www.blueridgeheritage.com/heritage/cherokee/cherokee-history/trail-of-tears

Character Names

The names of the character are taken from the Cherokee, Choctaw, Chickasaw, Abenaki, and Sioux.

Cherokee Names/Words

- **Ahyoka:** Kisosen's granddaughter; a Cherokee name meaning 'she brought happiness'

- **Ghigau:** Chief Yanegwa's wife; a Cherokee name meaning 'beloved woman'

- **Hialeah:** Kisosen's daughter-in-law; a Cherokee name meaning 'beautiful meadow'

- **Leotie:** a woman in the village; a Cherokee name meaning 'flower of the prairie'

- **Yanegwa:** the chief of the village; a Cherokee name meaning 'big bear'

Choctaw Names/Words

- **Acheba:** Kisosen's granddaughter's cornhusk doll; Choctaw for 'to be mischievous'

- **Mali humma:** the story antagonist; Choctaw meaning 'blow red'

- **Shikoba:** a child in the village; Choctaw for 'feather'

- **Tanampi:** Mali humma's brother; Choctaw for 'to be hostile; to be at war'

- **Winona:** Mali humma's daughter; Choctaw for daughter

Chickasaw Names/Words

- **Hashi:** is Chickasaw for sun

- **Itanale:** Kisosen's birth name; Chickasaw for 'I understand'

- **Losa:** a man in the village; Chickasaw for 'black'

- **Malili:** a man in the village; Chickasaw for 'he runs'

- **Onsi:** a man in the village; a Chickasaw name meaning 'eagle'

- **Shotek:** Mali humma's son; a Chickasaw name meaning 'sky'

Abenaki Names/Words

- **Kisosen:** sun bringer; taken from Abenaki tribal mythology. Kisosen is the solar deity, an eagle whose wings opened to create the day, and closed to cause the nighttime[7]

Sioux Names/Words

- **Chaska:** Kisosen's son; a Sioux name given to the first son born

---

[7] Found on many websites including:
http://www.warpaths2peacepipes.com/native-american-symbols/sun-symbol.htm

What's Accurate?

Most of the cultural information about the tribe in this story adheres to the facts I could find about the Cherokee of that time period.

The description of the village, dwellings, palisade, and tribal fields is accurate according to some sources. Others offer different descriptions of villages and housing.

The crops grown and description of the farming technique used is accurate as described in many references.[8] The food eaten by the tribe is consistent with southeastern tribes at that time. The clothing described also matches what I could find in historical references.

The weapons described, how they were made, and how they were used is accurate. Construction largely depended on what was available. I've made inferences about available materials as needed.

The burial ritual depicted in the story adheres to the traditions described on several Cherokee websites.[9,10] Death rituals varied widely in different

---

[8] Southeastern Agriculture. Native American Netroots. Found in May 2016 at: http://nativeamericannetroots.net/diary/953

[9] Cherokee funerary rites: death, mourning and purification. Cherokee by blood. Found in May, 2016 at: http://cherokeebyblood.com/Cherokee_by_blood/Funerary.html

[10] J.M. Clark. Burial Traditions of the Cherokee Indians. Demand Media. Found in May 2016 at: http://classroom.synonym.com/burial-traditions-cherokee-indians-7272.html

geographic regions, though. Some Native Americans buried their dead. Some piled rocks on the bodies. Others cremated bodies. Some even left the bodies for animals to pick clean and then retrieved the bones later for burial. I was not able to verify which traditions the Cherokee in the Asheville, NC area in the mid-1700's actually followed.

I also could not find details about how the Cherokee of that time period hunted bear, so I used information about bear hunting and skinning from modern literature to construct a plausible series of events.

The way the Cherokee dealt with criminals and murderers in the 1800's is very interesting. I found a document in the Library of Congress titled "Laws: The Cherokee Nation & C." This text details the laws established by a National Cherokee Council in the North Carolina area starting in 1808, along with a description of some cases and findings that led to new laws.[11] Here's an interesting passage in this document:

> *Be it known, also,* That should it so happen that a brother, forgetting his natural affection, should raise his hand in anger and kill his brother, he shall be accounted guilty of murder and suffer accordingly,

[11] Library of Congress. Laws of the Cherokee Nation in the early 1800s. Found in June 2016 at:
http://r.search.yahoo.com/_ylt=AwrBTz59Q2RXg5IAWDZXNyoA;_ylu=X3oDMTE ybWxyMG0wBGNvbG8DYmYxBHBvcwMzBHZ0aWQDQDQjE5MTBfMQRzZWMDc3l-/RV=2/RE=1466217469/RO=10/RU=http%3a%2f%2fwww.loc.gov%2flaw%2fhel p%2famerican-indian-consts%2fPDF%2f28014183.pdf/RK=0/RS=BmE1LOUAqAuBpufnv6S_DfP23sg-

and if a man has a horse stolen, and overtakes the thief and should his anger be so great as to cause him to kill him, let his blood remain on his own conscience, but no satisfaction shall be demanded for his life from his relatives or the clan he may belong to.

By order of the seven clans.

> T U R T L E AT HOME,
>
> Speaker of Council.
>
> Approved.—BLACK FOX, Principal Chief
>
> PATH KILLER, Sec'd
>
> TOOCHALER.
>
> CHARLES HICKS, Secretary to the Council.
>
> Oostanallah, April 10, 1810.

Here's another interesting entry from 1822 about how murderers were dealt with.

> ARTICLE 6th. If any subject of the Cherokee nation, should commit murder and run into the Creek nation, the Cherokees will make application to the Creeks to have the murderer killed, and when done, the Cherokee nation will give the man who killed the murderer, $200.
>
> ARTICLE 7th. If any subject of the Creek nation, should commit murder and run to the Cherokees, the Creeks will make application to the Cherokees to have the murderer killed, and when done the Creek nation will give the man who killed the murderer $200.
>
> ARTICLE 8th. If any Cherokees, should come over the line and commit murder or theft on the

Creeks, the Creeks will make a demand of the
Cherokees for satisfaction.

ARTICLE 9th. If any Creeks should come over the
line and commit murder or theft on the Cherokees,
the Cherokees will make a demand of the Creeks
for satisfaction.

The "Cherokee by Blood" website describes
similar laws. "Cherokee had tough laws to deal with
crime. Homicide was one of the worst crimes. When
both aggressor and victim were Cherokee, two
Cherokee clans would confront one another to settle
the matter by the customary rules of domestic law.
Blood revenge was a question of harmony, not
necessarily of a vendetta. If a member from one clan
killed the member of another, then balance must be
restored. Blood revenge was considered very sacred
and was carried out under the utmost sincerity."[12]

Lastly, the Cherokee prayers used in the story as
is, or slightly modified, were taken from several
different websites.[13] The sites do not list the time
period or location from which the prayer originates.

---

[12] Justice. Cherokee by blood. Found in May 2016 at:
http://www.cherokeebyblood.com/Cherokee_by_blood/Justice.html

[13] Prayer on p. 11 based on Prayer to the Sun at Litha;
http://paganwiccan.about.com/od/lithaprayers/qt/SunPrayerLitha.htm

Cherokee prayer on p. 64-65 based on one found at:
http://www.worldhealingprayers.com/2.html

Cherokee prayer on p. 71-72 found at: http://lightworkers.org/node/19539

Cherokee prayer on p.100 found at: http://lightworkers.org/node/19539

What is not Accurate?

In this story there are some significant inconsistencies with the Cherokee culture that must be acknowledged.

Marriage and Family Clans

In several historical references, it is said that it was forbidden for Cherokee to marry within their own tribe. Also, "when a Cherokee maiden selected a husband, he became a member of his wife's clan."[14] According to the North Carolina Museum of History, the Cherokee followed a matrilineal kinship system. In this type of system, "a person is related *only* to people on his mother's side. His relatives are those who can be traced through a woman. In this way a child is related to his mother, and through her to his brothers and sisters. He also is related to his mother's mother (grandmother), his mother's brothers (uncles), and his mother's sisters (aunts). The child is not related to the father, however. The most important male relative in a child's life is his mother's brother."[15]

In this story, the Kisosen is the oldest male in a long family line where the role is passed down from father to son. In this story, the Kisosen's son, Chaska,

---

[14] Found in May, 2016 at:
http://www.aboutnorthgeorgia.com/ang/The_Cherokee

[15] Cherokee Women. Found on June 17, 2016 at:
http://www.learnnc.org/lp/editions/nchist-twoworlds/1882

has married, but his wife has joined the Kisosen's family. If the tribe in the story were, in fact Cherokee, this would be inconsistent with the matrilineal culture of the North Carolina Cherokee tribes.

The Role of the Kisosen

The term "Kisosen" (Kee-zos-en) actually comes from Abenaki mythology. The Abenaki is a Native American tribe located in the northeastern United States. The Kisosen, a solar deity, was one of the tribe's Ancient Age beings. It is described as an eagle whose wings opened to create the day, and closed to cause the night.[16] This being was a god - not a person.

There is absolutely no evidence that the Cherokee or any southeastern tribe had a role for a tribal member as described in this story. This is completely fictional.

Two of the seven sacred ceremonies of the ancient Cherokee celebrated the first new moon of the spring and fall, but there were no ceremonies or festivals celebrating the sun.[17] There were several indigenous people, mostly located in the American

---

[16] Abenaki mythology. Found in February, 2016 at: http://www.thefullwiki.org/Abenaki_mythology

[17] Seven Sacred Cherokee Ceremonies. Ceremonies of the Cherokee. Found in June 2016 at: http://www.echotacherokeewolfclan.com/id1.html

Great Plains, who performed a Sun Dance.[18] The ceremony usually included a tribal gathering to pray for healing and the commitment of personal sacrifices to benefit the community.[19]

The Sun as the Primary Cherokee God

It is also not accurate to claim that the Cherokee, or any tribe in that region of the United States, viewed the sun as their primary God. According to sources, the central Cherokee God was the Great Spirit, the one who presided over all things and created the Earth.[20] There were also a set of venerated spirits, but none were the sun.[21]

---

[18] Encyclopedia of the Great Plains. Sun Dance. Found in June 2016 at: http://plainshumanities.unl.edu/encyclopedia/doc/egp.rel.046

[19] Wikipedia. Sun Dance. Found in June 2016 at: https://en.wikipedia.org/wiki/Sun_Dance

[20] Important Cherokee Mythological Figures. Found in June 2016 at: http://www.native-languages.org/cherokee-legends.htm

[21] Spirits and Beings of the Cherokee. Found in June 2016 at: http://mdiw.weebly.com/cherokee-indian-spirits-and-beings.html

Special Thanks

A special thanks to Deborah McClellan, Gertrud Bonam, and Joyce Felstehausen for their reviews and edits.

A big thanks to Bonnie Michel for the amazing book cover and map. See her website at: www.coroflot.com/bonniemichel.

And, a giant thanks to my sons, Max and Erik, for their encouragement and interest in the story, and for helping me to flesh out the details.

About the Author

Kris Felstehausen is an Instructional Designer, Learning Project Manager, speaker and author, and the Principal Consultant of *Felste Learning Works, LLC.*

She has a Masters in Music Theory from Northwestern University, a masters in Training and Performance Improvement from Capella University, and half of an MBA from DePaul University.

Kris is an avid organic gardener and inline speedskater and lives with her husband and two sons in Palatine, Illinois, a suburb of Chicago.

Visit her website/blog at: **FelsteLearningWorks.com**

63889041R00076

Made in the USA
Charleston, SC
16 November 2016